STACEY McGILL, SUPER SITTER

**Other books by
Ann M. Martin**

Rachel Parker, Kindergarten Show-off
Eleven Kids, One Summer
Ma and Pa Dracula
Yours Turly, Shirley
Ten Kids, No Pets
Slam Book
Just a Summer Romance
Missing Since Monday
With You and Without You
Me and Katie (the Pest)
Stage Fright
Inside Out
Bummer Summer

BABY-SITTERS LITTLE SISTER series
THE BABY-SITTERS CLUB mysteries
THE BABY-SITTERS CLUB series

STACEY McGILL, SUPER SITTER

Ann M. Martin

AN
APPLE
PAPERBACK

SCHOLASTIC INC.
New York Toronto London Auckland Sydney

Cover art by Hodges Soileau

No part of this publication may be reproduced in whole or in part, or stored in a retrieval system, or transmitted in any form or by any means, electronic, mechanical, photocopying, recording, or otherwise, without written permission of the publisher. For information regarding permission, write to Scholastic Inc., 555 Broadway, New York, NY 10012.

ISBN 0-590-22878-1

12 11 10 9 8 7 6 5 4 3 2 1   6 7 8 9/9 0 1/0

Printed in the U.S.A.   40

First Scholastic printing, February 1996

*The author gratefully acknowledges
Suzanne Weyn
for her help in
preparing this manuscript.*

STACEY McGILL, SUPER SITTER

CHAPTER 1

"Hurry! Run!" I told Robert. He grabbed my hand and together we raced down Slate Street.

As we ran hand in hand (or should I say glove in glove?), Robert smiled at me, which always just knocks me out.

Robert and I have been going together for awhile now, but I still can't believe it. He is the best. I enjoy every second we spend together.

We ran until we reached my front door. Panting, we stopped to catch our breath. The frozen winter afternoon was so cold that smokey mist puffed out of our mouths. "That worked," Robert said, laughing. "I'm not so cold anymore."

I'd warmed up, too, which was why I'd suggested running in the first place. "Let's get inside," I said, fumbling in my bag for the keys to my front door. (It's so hard to find things while wearing woolen gloves!)

When I finally unlocked the door, it felt good to be inside my warm house. With a shiver I peeled off my hot pink parka. "Oh, my gosh!" I laughed as I tried to pull off my pink beret. The hat tugged at my blonde permed hair.

"Wow," Robert said. "Your house is so quiet."

I paused and listened. The only noise was the gentle *thunk* of the boiler as it kicked on. It *was* pretty silent. I guess I hadn't noticed before.

"Doesn't it give you the creeps?" Robert asked, taking off his jacket.

"No," I answered. "Why should it?"

"I'm just not used to coming home to an empty house, I suppose," Robert replied. "When I get home there's always someone around."

"Mom will be home at six," I told him. She works for Bellair's department store. She's a buyer, which means she decides what Bellair's will sell.

My dad was at his office in Manhattan. But I wouldn't see him for another week and a half. That's because my parents are divorced. Mom and I live here in Connecticut. Dad still lives in Manhattan, where I lived for most of my life.

As I led Robert into the kitchen, the phone rang. "Hello?" I said, snapping up the receiver.

"Stacey, it's Dad," my father's voice said from the other end.

"Dad, hi! What's up?"

"I just thought I'd call to see how you are. I figured you might be lonely there all alone till your mother gets home."

"Oh, I'm not alone. Robert's here with me," I told him.

There was silence on the other end of the phone. "Dad?" I asked. "Are you there?"

Dad coughed. "I'm here. Uh . . . is it all right with your mother if Robert's in the house when she's not around?" he asked in an anxious voice.

"Oh, sure," I told him honestly. "You've met Robert. He's cool. We're just going to do some homework here in the kitchen. That's Mom's rule. We stay in the kitchen."

"All right, I suppose," said Dad. "That's probably all right."

I opened the refrigerator and handed Robert a bottle of raspberry-flavored seltzer while Dad and I talked briefly about a Broadway musical he'd seen the night before. He loved it and said he'd be willing to see it again with me when I came down to visit. "Want to do Broadway with your old dad?" he teased.

3

"Absolutely. Get tickets!" I told him enthusiastically. I adore Manhattan, and my dad is really fun. So I love doing things in Manhattan with him. It's a great combination.

Don't get me wrong, I like Stoneybrook, Connecticut, where I live now. But it's not nearly as exciting as the city. I think I'll always be a city person at heart.

I said good-bye to Dad and hung up. "Yes!" I cheered, turning to Robert. "Broadway, here I come. Dad and I are going to see a musical. Broadway is *so* exciting. The last time we saw a show we had supper in this restaurant nearby and we sat next to these two men who were discussing what stars they wanted for a play they were producing. They were mentioning names like Keanu Reeves, Macaulay Culkin, and Winona Ryder. Dad and I didn't talk for the whole meal. We just sat there and eavesdropped. It was really cool."

"You really love the city, don't you?" Robert asked as I opened the fridge again and pulled out a bunch of raw carrots.

"Sure I do," I replied, peeling a carrot over the sink. I wasn't really hungry but I knew I'd better eat. You see, I'm diabetic and I can't let myself get too hungry. Being diabetic means eating a lot of small meals and healthy snacks throughout the day. And I do mean *healthy* snacks. Sugar can send my body into orbit.

Serious stuff. I could go into a coma, even die, if I cheat on treats. So I watch what I eat, test my blood sugar level regularly, and give myself insulin injections every day.

There's no doubt about it. Having diabetes is a major drag.

Having divorced parents is a drag, too.

But, hey, those are the facts of my life, so I might as well make the best of things. Most of the time I don't let the divorce or the diabetes get me down.

"Want a carrot?" I asked, turning back to Robert.

"No, thanks."

Robert sat at the kitchen table. "Do you think you'll move back to the city when you're older?"

"I don't know," I admitted. "Maybe. Probably."

Robert sighed comically. "You'll leave all us country folk behind and go for the glamour," he teased.

"You're not exactly Farmer Rob," I pointed out as I sat beside him.

"I know, but I wouldn't like living in the city. I've only been there a few times and it seemed so noisy and big."

"Who cares about a little noise? And the bigness makes it exciting," I countered.

"No, the city isn't for me."

"I bet I could make a city lover out of you," I said, lightly squeezing his hand. "You just haven't seen the good parts yet. You need someone like me to guide you. For example, during the day Broadway looks sort of seedy but at night, when it's all lit up, it's magic."

"I've never even *been* to Broadway, Stacey."

"Well, then someday we'll go. Together," I said. "You'll love it."

"I don't know." Robert shook his head. "I don't think we'll ever agree about this one."

"We could," I said optimistically. "Once I give you the Stacey McGill super city tour you'll be as big a fan as I am. Oh, Robert, I wish you could see the city the way I do. It's so amazing. Every corner has some interesting discovery. You know, we like almost the same things. That's why I'm so sure you'd like the city if you gave it a chance."

"Oh, forget it," Robert said with a laugh. "I'll stay here in Stoneybrook and say that I once knew supermodel Stacey McGill."

I smiled, embarrassed but pleased. "I doubt it."

"You could be," Robert insisted. "You're pretty enough. You're more than pretty, you're beautiful. You already look like a model."

"Thanks," I said.

I don't think I'd want to be a model. It

sounds boring. I'll probably do something with math, which I'm really good at. But I was very happy that Robert thought I could be a supermodel if I wanted to be. "That's really nice to hear," I added.

Robert leaned forward, bringing his face closer to mine.

And then . . . the phone rang.

Robert laughed and pulled back away from me. "Better get it."

Rolling my eyes, I stood up and answered the phone. "Hello?"

"Can we afford more glue?" It was Kristy. I know her voice.

"Hi, Kristy. And how are *you*?" I teased.

"Sorry. Hi. Do we have enough money for glue? Mary Anne and I are at the mall. I was thinking it would be fun to make valentines with the kids but we need glue. Can we afford it?"

"How much glue are you buying?" I asked.

"Let me ask Mary Anne," said Kristy.

I suppose I should explain. I'm treasurer of a business called the Baby-Sitters Club (or BSC, for short). Kristy is the president and Mary Anne is the secretary. I'll tell you more about it later.

Kristy got back on the phone. "Mary Anne says five bottles of glue should do it. They're a dollar fifty each."

I did a quick mental tally of the dues I'd collected, and subtracted the club expenses we still had to pay out. I added the dues I'd collect next Monday to that sum. "Go for it," I told Kristy.

"Thanks," she replied. "See you tomorrow."

"That was Kristy," I told Robert as I hung up. "She wanted to know if we could afford glue."

"She's the president. Why doesn't she just go ahead and buy it?" Robert asked.

"You know Kristy," I said. "She does *everything* by the book."

Thanks to Kristy, the romantic mood between Robert and me was broken. We opened our math books and started going over our homework. We had moved on to computer science homework by the time I heard Mom come through the front door. "Hi, you guys," she said cheerfully, rubbing her hands to warm up as she entered the kitchen.

"Hi, Mrs. McGill," Robert said.

"Hi, Mom. How was work?" I asked.

Mom started taking food for dinner out of the cupboards. "Zooey. Can you believe we're already ordering summer clothing from the factories?"

"That's encouraging," I said. "It means spring *will* come someday."

"I know what you mean," Mom said. "It sure seems far away right now."

Robert and I worked for another half hour until he had to go home for dinner. "So long, Mrs. McGill. 'Bye, Stacey."

" 'Bye." I walked him to the door, then returned to the kitchen.

Mom handed me a head of lettuce and I began breaking it up into the large wooden salad bowl. I love this time of day when Mom and I prepare supper together. We talk about the day's events and how we feel about things that have happened. I'm lucky to have such an understanding mom. I can discuss anything with her. She's a parent but she's also a friend. We do a lot of things together and usually have a great time. Since the divorce I think Mom has been kind of lonely, so she looks forward to the time we spend together, too.

"Mom, can you believe Robert has never been to a Broadway play?" I asked thoughtfully.

Mom smiled. "A lot of people have never been to Broadway."

"I bet he would love it," I said. "Especially a musical."

Suddenly I had a brilliant idea. Robert's birthday was next month. I'd been racking my brain trying to think of the perfect gift for him. So far, I'd come up blank. But now I had it!

"I'm going to take Robert to a Broadway musical for his birthday!" I told Mom excitedly.

"Nice idea, Stacey, but have you checked out the price of a ticket lately?" Mom asked. "They're awfully expensive. Two decent seats will probably cost you over a hundred dollars."

I swallowed hard. I hadn't realized it was *that* expensive. But I really wanted to take him. I knew he'd have a great time, and it might even change his opinion of the city.

"I'll talk to Mary Anne," I told Mom. "I'll tell her I want as many baby-sitting jobs as possible." Mary Anne is in charge of assigning the jobs.

I was determined to show Robert the time of his life in New York City. I'd need the money fast, though, so I could be sure to get good tickets.

I couldn't wait until the next club meeting. I was ready, willing, and able to earn as much money as I could in the shortest amount of time possible.

CHAPTER 2

As I walked to our Wednesday afternoon BSC meeting, I was psyched to earn money. I crossed my fingers that the phone would ring and ring and ring for the entire half hour with customers calling in need of a sitter.

Of course, I couldn't just gobble up all the jobs. That wouldn't be fair. But I hoped everyone would be super busy with other activities so no one would mind if I took most of the baby-sitting assignments.

Maybe I should back up a bit so you have some clue as to what I'm talking about. The Baby-sitters Club is a group of friends who meet for half an hour three times a week. During those meetings we take calls from parents who need baby-sitters. That way, instead of making seven different phone calls in search of a sitter, they can make one phone call and get in touch with seven qualified sitters at one time.

Neat idea, huh?

It's more like a business than a club, really. But we call it a club because we're all friends as well as coworkers.

The BSC was Kristy Thomas's idea. She thought it up one day while watching her mother go crazy trying to find a sitter for her younger brother. She told her great idea — of having one number where people could reach several sitters — to her best friend Mary Anne Spier. They told their other friend Claudia Kishi and she suggested I join them, too. Claudia has her own phone *and* her own phone number, so that was perfect for us. We put up fliers advertising our business all over Stoneybrook.

The club was an instant success!

It was such a success that we needed more help. That's when we invited Dawn Schafer, who'd just moved here from California, to join.

Things went great for a while, then my dad's company transferred him back to New York City. I felt all mixed up when that happened. I love Manhattan (as you already know). But I'd also made close friends here in Stoneybrook. I hated leaving them. There was nothing I could do about it, though. Off we went, back to Manhattan.

While I was gone, BSC business continued

to boom. They needed more help and fast. That was when Kristy recruited Mallory Pike and Jessi Ramsey.

They're eleven, which is why they're junior officers. (The rest of us are thirteen.) As junior officers they baby-sit during the afternoons, and at night only for their own siblings. That leaves the other members free to take the evening jobs, so it works out well.

Anyway, getting back to the club history — things were not going so great for me in Manhattan. Mom and Dad started fighting all the time. Before too long I got the bad news: divorce.

Mom decided to move *back* to Stoneybrook. And I had to decide which parent to live with. Was that ever a tough one! But after many sleepless nights, I picked Stoneybrook.

Luckily the BSC needed me back. The club was growing like crazy.

Then something unexpected happened. Dawn decided she wanted to visit her father and brother in California. (Her parents are divorced, too.) Her visit went great — too great. When she came home she really missed being in California.

Around then I started seeing a lot of Robert. It was a confusing time for me because Robert hangs with a whole different crowd of kids. In the beginning, I thought they were much cooler than my BSC friends. I dropped out of the club for a while to become part of their group.

That left the club shorthanded. They called Shannon Kilbourne, who sometimes filled in as an associate member, and asked her to be a full-time member. That didn't work out too well because Shannon is so involved in after-school activities that she just didn't have the time for many baby-sitting jobs.

In the meantime I discovered that my new friends might be cool, but they weren't real friends. I asked to join the club again and everyone made me feel welcome (eventually). It was lucky I came back, because not long after that, Dawn decided to return to California — for good.

That left the club one member short once again. Fortunately, around that time Abby and Anna Stevenson moved into Kristy's neighborhood. Kristy invited both twins — who are also thirteen — to join. Anna said no, but Abby said yes. Now, with Abby here, things are running smoothly again.

So, that's a brief history of the BSC.

I arrived at Claudia's house and pulled open the front door. On Mondays, Wednesdays, and Fridays — which are club meeting days — Claudia's mom leaves the door open so we can go right up to Claud's room. We always hold meetings here, which is why she's the vice-president.

"Hi," I said as I entered Claudia's bedroom. Kristy and Claud were already there. Naturally, Claudia was there because she lives there. Kristy is often early because she's the president of the club and she takes it super seriously.

"We bought the glue," Kristy reported from her usual seat, Claudia's director's chair.

"Good," I replied. I was about to bounce onto Claudia's bed (*my* usual spot) when I stopped short. "Ahh!" I cried, waving my arms in the air to regain my balance. "What's all this?" Claudia's bed was strewn with pieces of red construction paper, doilies, colored foil, and markers. "It's stuff for making valentines," Claudia explained as she wiggled her fingers into a bag of peanut M&Ms. "I'm putting together valentine craft kits."

I should have known making valentines was a project Claudia would dive right into. Anything artistic attracts her like a magnet. She paints, sculpts, sketches, makes prints, tie-dyes, makes jewelry, and even designs her own clothing sometimes.

Her creativity overflows to her unique fashion sense. For instance, today she wore a long-sleeved tie-dyed shirt that she'd dyed herself. Under it she had on black leggings onto which

15

she'd sewn patches of the tie-dyed material. Her silky, long black hair was tied back with a matching tie-dyed scrunchy.

Claudia looks great in her unusual outfits. It doesn't hurt that she's completely gorgeous. She's Japanese-American with the greatest hair, smoothest skin, prettiest dark almond eyes, and a knockout smile.

I can't understand how she can look so great and eat the way she does. Claudia is a total junk food nut. Her parents don't approve of her eating habits so she stashes junk food all over her room. You have to be careful where you sit; you might be squashing a pack of Twinkies or a bag of Doritos.

Claudia's biggest problem is school. She just can't seem to find anything to like about it other than art class. She's so involved with her art that other classes don't interest her. Considering that her older sister Janine is a genius (with a super I.Q. score to prove it), Claudia's parents are shocked by (and sometimes unhappy about) Claudia's dislike of school. They're on her back to study all the time. Claudia tries but schoolwork just isn't for her.

"Claudia, it's almost time for the meeting. You better start organizing this stuff," Kristy said. "Do you have the sandwich bags?"

"I have wax paper bags," said Claudia, taking a cardboard box from her top drawer. "They're more biodegradable." She opened the box, pulled out some bags, and started sorting equal amounts of doilies, red paper, and everything else into each bag. "Putting together these valentine kits was a great idea," she told Kristy.

"Thanks," said Kristy. "I figured it would be fun for the kids."

That's Kristy, queen of the great idea. She's not shy about sharing her ideas, either. In fact, she's not shy about anything. We seldom have to wonder what Kristy is thinking. She's always happy to tell us.

Kristy doesn't look particularly impressive. She's petite with straight, shoulder-length brown hair. She's not especially interested in clothing. Jeans, sneakers, and a T-shirt or sweatshirt are her usual attire.

But, in Kristy's case, looks are deceiving. Kristy is very impressive. She has a big, bold personality. Sometimes her bossiness can be a bit of a pain, but she keeps this club running like clockwork. She's also got a good heart and is a loyal friend. Besides, Kristy can be a lot of fun. Some of her great ideas involve activities — such as sleepovers, plays, and pizza parties — that are a blast.

Kristy's life hasn't always been easy. Her father just walked out on her family after her younger brother was born. That left her mother to take care of Kristy, her younger brother David Michael, and her two older brothers Charlie and Sam. Her mother managed well enough, though I suppose it must have been hard. Then, one day, Kristy's mom met this guy named Watson Brewer and soon they fell in love.

And Watson turned out to be a millionaire.

Before long, wedding bells rang and Kristy's family moved across town to Watson's mansion. You got it — mansion! That big mansion came in handy, too, because Kristy's family started to grow. First, Watson and Kristy's mom adopted a baby girl named Emily Michelle who was born in Vietnam. (She's two and a half now.) Then Kristy's grandmother, Nannie, moved in to help look after Emily Michelle. Kristy also acquired two younger stepsiblings, Karen, who is seven, and Andrew, who is four. They live at Kristy's every other month. When you add assorted cats, dogs, and goldfish, it makes for a pretty busy household.

"Am I on time?" asked Mary Anne, rushing breathlessly into the room. She checked Claudia's digital clock. "Five twenty-five. Phew!" she said.

Kristy is a stickler for punctuality. Our meetings start at five-thirty sharp. If we're late we get the Kristy Look, an icy stare of disapproval.

Mary Anne caught her breath and pulled the club record book from her backpack, preparing for our meeting. The record book contains everything she needs to know in order to schedule jobs. All of our schedules as well as the names and phone numbers of our regular clients are carefully noted. Any other important information is in there too, such as clients' allergies or special needs. As club secretary, Mary Anne keeps track of it all and, amazingly, has never made a scheduling mistake.

"Dawn called last night," Mary Anne reported. "Isn't it strange to think that she went to the beach yesterday, while we were here freezing?"

As she spoke about Dawn (the club member who left and went to California), Mary Anne was smiling, but I had to wonder how she was really feeling. She and Dawn are very close. She took Dawn's departure the hardest of all. You see, they aren't only great friends, but they are stepsisters.

Dawn and Mary Anne became stepsisters by reuniting their parents, who had once been high-school sweethearts. While browsing through an old yearbook, they discovered that Dawn's mother had dated Mary Anne's father when they were in high school. But then Dawn's mom went to California to go to col-

19

lege, where she met and married Dawn's father. Back in Stoneybrook, Mary Anne's father married someone else — Mary Anne's mother.

Got that so far?

Anyway, as you know, Dawn's parents divorced. Her mother came back to Stoneybrook with Dawn and Jeff, Dawn's younger brother.

Since Mary Anne's mother died when she was a baby, her father was raising Mary Anne by himself. So, as you may have figured out by now, both Dawn's mother and Mary Anne's father were free to get back together again.

After much coaxing from their daughters, Mary Anne's dad, Richard, and Dawn's mom, Sharon, began to date, then eventually married. Mary Anne and her father moved in with Dawn and her mother. (By then, Jeff had already moved back to California.)

Becoming a new family had its definite and unexpected pitfalls. For example, Dawn, who is tall with long white-blonde hair, has strong opinions about a lot of things, including food. She can't stand junk food or red meat. Mary Anne, on the other hand, feels ill at the sight of barbecued tofu. But they ironed out their differences and everything seemed to be going great. That's why it was so shocking when Dawn announced her decision to move back to California to live with her brother, her dad, and her dad's new wife, Carol. It was something she felt she really had to do. I sympathized with her because she really agonized over the decision.

I think Mary Anne is still getting over it, although she tries to have a good attitude. She's very sensitive and cries easily. The up side of her sensitivity is that she's a great friend, really tuned in to other people's feelings. The down side is that her feelings are easily hurt.

You can tell Mary Anne is sweet just by looking at her. She's petite, like Kristy, with big brown eyes that look even bigger now that she's cut her brown hair short.

Even though Mary Anne is quiet and shy she was the first one of us to have a steady boyfriend. Logan Bruno is a great guy. He has sandy blond hair and a southern accent left over from when he used to live in Kentucky. He's an associate club member, which means he sometimes takes fill-in baby-sitting jobs when the rest of us are booked.

Our other associate member is Shannon, as I've already mentioned. I like her a lot, even though she attends private school and is so busy that I don't see much of her. She's cute with curly blonde hair, the bluest eyes, and high cheekbones. She lives near Kristy and has two younger sisters.

I glanced at the clock and watched it turn

from 5:29 to 5:30. Uh-oh. Abby, Jessi, and Mallory were still missing. They were doomed to get the Look.

Kristy checked the clock and frowned deeply. "All right, we might as well get started," she grumbled, obviously unhappy to have three members missing. "Mary Anne, would you check the record book and — "

"We're here!" Mallory interrupted, flying into the room just ahead of Jessi.

"You're late," said Kristy.

"Are not," Mal protested as she looked at the clock. At that very second, the clock switched to 5:31. "It was five-thirty when we walked through that door."

"She's right," I said.

Kristy scowled. "I suppose," she admitted grudgingly. Kristy doesn't like us to cut it that close.

Mallory smiled at Jessi and the two best friends slapped a high five.

I love to watch Jessi and Mallory together. In some ways they're both so sensible and grown-up, and then — in an instant — they can seem like real kids. (Right now was one of those instants. They were jumping around and slapping one another high fives behind their backs and in every conceivable way.)

Jessi is an excellent ballerina. She studies at a dance school in Stamford (which is the nearest city to Stoneybrook). She's already performed in a few professional productions. She was the lead in one of her ballet school productions.

I'm sure Jessi will be a famous ballerina someday. She works hard and is very talented. She even *looks* like a dancer with her long, graceful arms and legs. Mostly she wears her black hair in a tight bun like dancers do. Since that hairstyle leaves nothing to the imagination, it's lucky for Jessi she has such a pretty face with clear skin and large dark eyes.

Here's a coincidence. Jessi lives in my old house, the one we moved out of when we returned to Manhattan. Just like my family, her family came here because her dad's company transferred him. The move was hard for Jessi for all the normal reasons that moves are hard on kids, and for one extra reason. Jessi's family is African-American. They used to live in an integrated neighborhood, but Stoneybrook is mostly European-American. (That's a phrase I heard someone use on the radio today.)

Some people in Stoneybrook were totally obnoxious to Jessi's family just because of their skin color. (People can be such jerks sometimes!) Fortunately *that* craziness has blown over, and the Ramseys are happily settled in now with good friends and neighbors. Jessi's family consists of her mom and dad; a younger sister, Becca, who is eight; and her baby brother, Squirt, who is almost two. Jessi's aunt Cecelia also lives with them. She takes care of Squirt and Becca while Mr. and Mrs. Ramsey work.

Jessi has a pretty big family, but it's nothing compared to Mallory's family. The Pikes have eight kids! There are the triplets, Adam, Byron, and Jordan, who are ten, then comes Vanessa (nine), Nicky (eight), Margo (seven), and Claire, who is only five. They live in a busy house on Slate Street.

The size of Mal's family explains why she's such a good baby-sitter. She sure knows about little kids. Being the oldest has made her very responsible, too. But Mal has her dreams. She wants to be an author-illustrator of children's books. She's talented, too.

Mal says she doesn't want to have her picture on the back cover of any of her books because she can't stand her looks. I think she's too hard on herself, though. Mal has curly reddish-brown hair, glasses, and braces. Mal disagrees, but in my opinion she's cute.

"I need the club notebook," said Mal. "I have a *lot* to write about my last job, sitting for the Barretts and the DeWitts. Those kids are possibly crazier than *my* brothers and sisters." The club notebook is a kind of diary where we record our baby-sitting experiences. (Mal loves writing in it, the rest of us don't.) It's very helpful because it's a place to read about client families and keep up with what's happening with them.

"Here it is," said Claudia, handing Mallory the notebook.

"Where's that Abby?" Kristy bellowed.

As I mentioned, Abby is the newest member of the club. She's slim with long, curly brown hair and brown eyes. I like her because she's sharp and very funny.

Just then Abby rushed in. Usually she gets a ride here with Kristy, but today she must have come from somewhere else. Her walk is always brisk and energy-charged, but she wasn't breathless. She didn't instantly check the clock like the rest of us do.

"Abby, it's five-thirty-three," Kristy pointed out.

"Oh, good, I made it on time," Abby said with a smile.

I took a deep breath. I had to admire her nerve. She knows full well that Kristy doesn't consider five-thirty-three on time.

Kristy shot her the dreaded Look.

We all cringed.

Abby didn't even seem to notice. She flipped back her curls and sat at the edge of Claudia's bed.

"Try to be here exactly at five-thirty next time," Kristy said in an icy voice.

Abby raised her eyebrows quizzically. "Are you sure that clock is exactly right? I mean, maybe it's a minute fast."

"It's not," Kristy said confidently.

"Well, I think you should call Greenwich, England, and check," Abby insisted. "That's where they set the exact time, isn't it?"

"This clock is right," Kristy grumbled.

I tried hard not to smile. Abby is originally from Long Island, which is close to the city. She has a lot of that big-city attitude my other city friends have. That attitude says, "No one is pushing me around." She has that same dry sense of humor, too.

Luckily, the tension was broken by the sound of the ringing phone. "Hello. Baby-sitters Club," Claudia answered, since she happened to be sitting nearest the phone. From the way she was talking, I could tell it wasn't one of our regular customers. She wrote information on a pad, then said, "I'll see who's available and call you right back." (That's how we always handle calls.)

Mary Anne already had the record book open on her lap.

"I'd like the job," I said before I'd even heard who it was for or when.

26

Mary Anne looked at me with a puzzled expression. "How do you even know you're free?" she asked.

"I don't care," I replied. "I'll cancel whatever I'm doing. I just really need to earn enough money to take Robert to a Broadway show for his birthday."

"It's a new family who just moved in," Claudia told Mary Anne and me. "Their name is Cheplin. Mrs. Cheplin wants a regular baby-sitter who can pick up her kids after school every afternoon and take care of them until she gets home from work at five-thirty."

"For how long?" asked Kristy.

"I don't know. Regularly, I guess," replied Claud.

"Well, I can't do it every single day, I have too much to do," said Abby.

"And I have art club," Claudia said.

"I'll have to coach the Krushers soon," said Kristy, who is the coach for a little kids' softball team called Kristy's Krushers.

"I have ballet," Jessi said.

"My parents wouldn't let me do it every day," Mallory said.

"Neither would mine," added Mary Anne. "And I wouldn't want to make that kind of commitment. Why don't we split the job up among us?"

"Wait a minute!" I cried. "I can do it. Call her back and say I'll do it. It doesn't sound hard and I want the money."

"All right," Mary Anne said with a worried expression. "If you're sure."

"Sure, I'm sure," I told her enthusiastically. I couldn't believe how lucky I was. I'd wanted a lot of work and I got it. Just like that. Unbelievable! Great!

At least, I thought it was great at the time.

CHAPTER 3

The Cheplins weren't easy to find. They live on Acorn Place, one of those twisting roads over by Burnt Hill Road, where Mary Anne lives. Near my house, the blocks all fall into straight lines, but over there they twist and turn and don't have any particular order that I can figure out.

By the time I reached the house that Thursday afternoon, I was fifteen minutes late. Despite the biting cold, I felt overheated and breathless from pedaling my bike up the steep hill leading to Acorn Place. The Cheplins' small house was brick with bright blue shutters. It was set on a thickly wooded hillside that led down to a stream. It looked cozy, like a house from a fairy tale.

Leaning my bike against a slate rock walkway at the front of the house, I walked down several stone steps and banged the brass front

29

door knocker that was shaped like a wood-pecker.

A heavyset woman with short brown hair and large blue-framed glasses opened the door. She was dressed casually in soft slacks and an oversized tunic top. "Yes?" she said with a puzzled expression. "What can I do for you?"

"I'm Stacey," I said. "Sorry I'm late. I rode right past the turnoff on Burnt Hill Road and took a few other wrong turns."

The woman blinked hard and seemed to study me.

"Are you Mrs. Cheplin?" I asked in a small voice, suddenly worried that I was at the wrong house.

"Yes, yes, I am," she said with a quick, embarrassed laugh. "Please come in, Stacey. I'm sorry. I don't mean to leave you standing in the cold. You just took me by surprise. I was expecting someone more . . . well . . . someone older."

"I'm thirteen," I said, in case she thought I was younger than that.

"I was really hoping for a high-school girl."

As I stepped inside the front hallway, I could see the small, narrow kitchen, which was set behind a brick wall. A sunny living room was off to the right, and in between the kitchen and living room was a hall with spiral stairs leading to the second floor.

It was a shadowy house, put together artistically with woven rugs, interesting cloth wall hangings, photographs, and original paintings everywhere.

It was also very cluttered. Magazines, stacks of papers, toys, blocks, videos, and notebooks were perched on every shelf and in every corner.

"I've had lots of sitting jobs," I told Mrs. Cheplin. "If you want, I can get you some references."

"Let's sit in here," she said, ushering me into the living room off the hallway. It was as cluttered as the hall, but a big window looking out on the woods let in patches of sunshine and a view of the woods.

Mrs. Cheplin scooped a toy fire truck off an overstuffed blue chair and nodded for me to sit. She sat at the end of the gray loveseat to the side of the chair. Still holding the toy truck, she leaned forward as she spoke to me. "You see, Stacey, I need someone who can be very responsible. Up until now I've been freelancing from home. I'm a photographer and book designer. But I've just taken a job as an art director for a magazine in Stamford and I really must have someone I can rely on."

"You can rely on me," I said confidently.

Mrs. Cheplin didn't look convinced. "I'm

sure you're a terrific sitter, Stacey," she said. "But I really do need someone more mature. I'm sorry, but — "

"Mrs. Cheplin," I interrupted. I wasn't going to let this great steady job slip out of my fingers so easily. Especially since I was sure I could handle it. "I bet I can get the job done for you. What exactly do you need?"

"Dana and Adam go to the Miller School," she said. I'd heard of that. It was a private school just outside Stoneybrook. "They have to be picked up at their school bus stop at three-fifteen sharp every day," she continued. "If no one is there the driver won't let them off and they'd be very upset."

"Believe me, I know about being punctual," I said, thinking of the excellent punctuality training I'd received from Kristy. "Our club meetings always start at five-thirty sharp. Our president, Kristy, insists that we're there on time."

Mrs. Cheplin adjusted her glasses. "Well, that's good. I'd also need you to help the kids with their homework, and after that to keep them busy with games and projects until I get home at five-thirty. I don't want them sitting around in front of the TV."

"No problem," I assured her. "I don't mind helping with homework. If they need math help, I'm in honors math at school. And I'll bring my Kid-Kit with me." I explained that a Kid-Kit is a box filled with art materials, books, games, puzzles, and lots of fun odds and ends. Every member of the BSC has her own and we use our club dues to keep them stocked.

Mrs. Cheplin nodded and I got the idea that the Kid-Kits had impressed her. "Your club certainly sounds well-organized," she commented.

"Oh, it is," I said. "You wouldn't believe how organized."

"As you can guess from looking around, I could use some organization *here*," Mrs. Cheplin said. "How would you feel about some light housekeeping?"

Instinctively, I could feel my nose start to wrinkle with distaste, but I forced myself to stop. "As long as it doesn't interfere with watching the children," I replied, which I thought was a lot better than making a disgusted face.

"That's true. It's hard to do both, which is why this place looks the way it does. But still . . . I was hoping to find someone who could give me a hand with it. Maybe this just isn't going to work out. Besides, I think you're just too young to deal with Dana."

"Why?" I asked. "Is she difficult?"

"No. She's a sweet eight-year-old. But she's just been diagnosed with diabetes and — "

"I have diabetes, too," I cut in.

Behind her glasses, Mrs. Cheplin's eyes widened in surprise. "You do?"

I nodded. "I've had it for a long time."

"But you seem so healthy and energetic. You must have the kind of diabetes you control simply through diet," she said, assuming I had a less severe form of diabetes than I have.

"Diet and insulin," I said.

Mrs. Cheplin folded her arms. "Really? And you rode your bike all the way up that hill?"

"Sure," I said. "As long as I take care of myself I can do anything other girls do."

"Then you know how important it is not to let Dana have sweets."

"Absolutely," I said. "She should snack, though. You don't want her blood sugar to get too low."

A thoughtful expression came across Mrs. Cheplin's face. "It might be good for Dana to get to know you," she said, leaning back and sliding her arms along the top of the couch. "It might be a very good thing for her. Why don't we try it for one week? If it seems to be working, we'll continue. If there are problems we'll chalk it up to experience and call it quits."

"Great!" I said enthusiastically. "I'm sure I can do it."

Then Mrs. Cheplin told me how much she

was willing to pay me and I nearly slid off the chair. It was almost twice as much as most baby-sitting jobs pay!

"When do I start?" I asked.

"I just had a thought," said Mrs. Cheplin, looking concerned again. "Do your parents know you're taking this job?"

"Not *this* job, but they know I baby-sit and it's cool with them."

"But this is every day," she pointed out. "Why don't you talk to them and give me a call tonight?"

Now *I* was worried. What if Mom said no?

"All right, I'll call you tonight," I told Mrs. Cheplin as I got up from the chair. I noticed a black-and-white photo of two children hanging on the wall. The girl had blunt cut, straight blonde hair. The line of bangs across her forehead skirted large, expressive eyes. The round-faced boy had wispy brown hair. He, too, had big eyes that shone mischievously.

"Those are my cuties," said Mrs. Cheplin. "They're good kids but they can be a handful. As I mentioned, Dana is eight. Adam is six."

"No problem. I'm used to kids, and they look really sweet," I said.

I left Mrs. Cheplin's house and climbed back on my bike. (Going downhill was definitely easier, but the turns were a little scary as the bike speeded faster and faster.) At the bottom

35

of Burnt Hill Road I spotted Mary Anne and Kristy in Mary Anne's front yard. They looked as if they were just about to go into the house.

"Hi!" Mary Anne called to me.

Slowing the bike, I turned up Mary Anne's driveway. "I just saw Mrs. Cheplin," I reported as I stood in the driveway straddling my bike.

"What were the kids like?" Mary Anne asked.

"I don't know. It was just an interview, not an actual job."

"Sounds serious," said Kristy. "Like more than just a baby-sitting job."

"It's a big time commitment," I said. "But other than that, it isn't any different."

Kristy shifted uneasily from side to side and shook her head. "I don't think you should take it."

"Why not?" I asked, my voice rising a bit.

"Well, because it's like we're losing another member. And just when everything was settled, too," Kristy said.

"How can you possibly look at it that way?" I asked.

"When will you be free to take baby-sitting jobs?" Kristy countered.

"I'll be *baby-sitting* every single day until five-thirty," I reminded her. "How much more of a baby-sitting club member can I be than that?"

"But you won't be able to take other jobs," Kristy argued.

"What's the difference?" I retorted.

"You're sitting until five-thirty?" said Mary Anne. "You won't be able to come to meetings then."

I grimaced. Meetings. "Oops, I forgot about meetings," I admitted sheepishly.

"You forgot about meetings!" Kristy exploded.

"For the moment," I said quickly. "Just for the moment. I could be there by quarter to six."

"Why bother? You won't be free to take any baby-sitting jobs anyway."

"Yes I will," I protested. "There's always Saturday and Sunday, which are our busiest times anyway."

"Will you want to baby-sit on weekends after sitting all week long?" Mary Anne asked doubtfully.

Probably not, I thought, but I didn't want to upset Kristy any more than she already was. "Sure," I said. "If you need me I'll just have to do it. That's all."

"We'll need you," said Kristy. "I guess it's all right if you come late to meetings. I hope everyone doesn't start doing it, though."

"Don't worry," Mary Anne told her. "She's coming late for a good reason."

"I'll be baby-sitting and I'll be at meetings, so you're not losing a member," I told Kristy.

"I hope not," she said sulkily. In a way, I couldn't blame her for worrying. With all the shifting around of club members lately she probably just wanted things to settle down and run smoothly for awhile.

"We were about to make some hot chocolate," Mary Anne told me. "Want to come in and have tea?"

"No, thanks," I said. "I have to get home. I want to run this job past Mom." I got on my bike and started pedaling down the driveway. "See you guys tomorrow!" I called over my shoulder.

"I hope your mother says no!" Kristy called after me.

Would she? I didn't think so. But I began pedaling faster, anxious to talk to her and find out her answer for sure.

CHAPTER 4

"It sounds terrific," Mom said when I told her about the job at the Cheplins'. "It's a commitment, though, you know."

"Yeah, but it's just two and a half hours a day," I pointed out. "What's the big deal?"

"All right, as long as you think you can handle it," she said.

I called Mrs. Cheplin right away and told her I was definitely interested in the job. "I start my job a week from this Monday," she said, sounding worried again. "I'll expect you to meet them at the bus that day. You won't forget, will you?"

"Absolutely not," I assured her. "I'll write it on the kitchen calendar in big letters."

As soon as I hung up, I *did* write it down, but I was sure I wouldn't forget. I'm pretty responsible about baby-sitting jobs. I certainly wouldn't leave two little kids stranded with no one to meet them at the bus.

The next day in school I was in a great mood. All I could think about was what play I'd take Robert to see. I figured I'd get Dad's suggestions when I saw him on the weekend.

I was also feeling good because I was looking forward to this evening. Robert and I were going to double date with Logan and Mary Anne. It was just a bowling date, but those are fun.

After lunch, Robert met me at my locker. "Got your bowling arm ready?" he asked with a smile.

"Yup," I replied, shutting the door to my locker. "I'm psyched. Mary Anne and Logan won't win again this time."

Robert reached out and took my hand as we began walking down the hall. "I don't know," he said lightly. "Last time they were really on a roll. *On a roll*, get it?"

I poked him playfully. "Very funny."

"I didn't exactly *score* with that joke, did I?" Robert continued.

"Don't *pin* me down," I joked back.

We stopped at a corner of the hall. "Well," said Robert. "Here's where I *split*."

"Oh, cut it out!" I laughed. "See you tonight."

"I'll be at your house at seven," Robert told me. "With time to *spare*."

"Aaaugh!" I cried, pretending to be exasperated. " 'Bye!"

That night as I dressed to go out, I felt optimistic about everything. I imagined sitting with Robert in a Broadway theater. At intermission he would turn to me and say something like, "Stacey, you were right. The city is great. I'm wild about it! Thanks for showing me how much fun it can be."

After I pulled on a pair of blue leggings and a long, bright pink sweater, I sat on the end of my bed and put on my new black leather ankle boots. I used a pick on my perm to fluff it out, then put on some mascara and pink lipstick. A pair of big hoop earrings finished the look. I went downstairs to wait for Robert.

"You look nice," said Mom just as the front doorbell rang.

"Thanks," I said, heading for the door.

Whenever I open the door to Robert I feel as if I'm seeing him for the first time. Each time, he seems just a little cuter than I remembered. "Hi," he said.

"Hi."

Mary Anne ran to the front door behind him. "Ready?" she asked. I saw that her father, who was driving us to the bowling alley, had just pulled into the driveway. I waved to Logan, who was in the backseat.

41

" 'Bye, Mom!" I said as I grabbed my parka.

"Have fun," she told me. "Be out front by nine-thirty."

Mom was picking us up. "We'll be there," I assured her.

Mr. Spier drove us to the bowling alley. We rented our shoes and didn't wait long for a free lane. Mary Anne and Logan were ready for us. They'd brought sharpened pencils for keeping score, and Logan had even borrowed his father's shiny blue-speckled bowling ball.

"We were just going easy on you last time," Robert told Logan. "This time we're ready."

"Why? Have you been practicing?" asked Logan as he tied his red-and-black bowling shoes.

Robert and I looked at one another and burst out laughing. We couldn't picture ourselves being so into bowling that we'd actually practice. "No!" I blurted out.

"But we've been practicing in our heads," Robert said, his eyes dancing mischievously. "Mental attitude counts for a lot."

"Okay, Mr. Spock," Logan teased. "Let's see if you can use the Vulcan mind meld to keep that ball out of the gutter."

Robert put one hand on a bowling ball and the other on his forehead. He closed his eyes and scrunched up his face as if he were concentrating hard. "No problem," he reported, opening his eyes again. "The bowling ball and I are one."

"One what?" Mary Anne asked as she wrote our names on the score sheets.

"One nut case." Logan laughed.

"You'll see," Robert said knowingly. "We're ready. Right, Stacey?"

"Yeah, *right*," I replied sarcastically. "We're ready."

As it turned out we did better than I expected. Maybe Robert was right about the power of the mind. I was in such a good mood that I bowled better than usual. I wonder if there was a connection. Throughout the game Robert and I were almost tied with Mary Anne and Logan.

"Whoa, guys!" Logan said admiringly. "That mind meld is working."

"You'd better have a talk with your dad's ball," Robert kidded. "Tell him it's time to get tough. Stacey and I are through fooling around with you. Now we're out to win this thing."

"In that case I need strength," Logan said. "I need a pizza break."

"Pizza sounds good," Robert agreed.

"They have those big soft pretzels here," I recalled enthusiastically. Pretzels are one of the snack foods I can have. The big baked kind reminds me of the city, where vendors sell them warm on street corners.

"I'll come help you carry the food back," Mary Anne said to Logan.

"Uh . . . no . . . one person from each team should go," Logan replied.

We all looked at him with puzzled expressions. "Why?" Mary Anne asked.

"Because . . . uh . . . uh . . . because that's fair. I mean, each team should have its members equally tired out," Logan said.

"Yeah, like walking to the food counter is *so* exhausting," Robert said drily.

Logan shrugged and grinned. "Hey, in a game this close who knows, it might make a difference."

"You're crazy," I laughed. "But I'll go with you."

Logan and I walked toward the food counter together. "Did that sound totally nuts?" Logan asked.

"Yes," I said.

"I just had to find a way to talk to you alone."

"What about?"

While the counterperson heated three pieces of pizza and a big pretzel, Logan told me what was on his mind. "I want to buy Mary Anne a ring for Valentine's Day," he said.

"How sweet!" I cried. "She'll love that."

"I want her to love it," Logan said, "but

that's what I'm worried about. I'm not sure I'll pick out a ring she'll love."

"You can always return it," I reminded him.

Logan made a face. "I know. It's not the same, though. It's much better if she loves the ring right off the bat."

"That's true," I agreed.

"Would you come shopping with me? You know Mary Anne's taste. I'd feel better if you helped me pick out the ring."

"Sure," I said. "When do you want to go?"

"I'll have the money by next week," Logan said. "How about then? We can go downtown right after school."

"Okay, I can — " I stopped short. I'd forgotten about my new job with the Cheplins. "Can't," I said. "I'll be working until five-thirty every night."

Logan looked disappointed.

"Why not ask Kristy to go with you?" I suggested. "She knows Mary Anne's taste as well as I do, maybe even better."

"That's a good idea," said Logan. "Okay. I'll ask her. This should be a great Valentine's Day. I'll have the ring, and I've made reservations at Chez Maurice."

"Chez Maurice!" I gasped, clasping my hands together excitedly. "How romantic!"

"I hope Mary Anne thinks so," said Logan.

"She will," I assured him. "Definitely."

I heard a timer beep and soon the guy behind the counter brought us our food. We bought some sodas (club soda for me) and returned to our lane.

"So, are you guys exhausted from your big trip to the food counter?" Robert asked.

"Totally," I said, taking a bite of my pretzel.

"Me too," said Logan. "See? So now it's fair."

After eating, we continued to play. We actually beat Logan and Mary Anne. Okay, so it was only by ten points, but I *did* get a couple of strikes, which is pretty good for me. Logan and Mary Anne won the next two games. Robert and I didn't really care. It was all just for fun.

By nine-thirty we were waiting outside for Mom. Good thing we only waited a minute or two because it was cold! It felt great to climb into the nice, warm car.

Mom dropped Logan off first, then Mary Anne.

"What were you and Logan talking about at the food counter?" Robert asked as soon as Mary Anne climbed out of the car. "I was watching and it looked serious."

"Not *that* serious," I told him as Mom pulled out of Mary Anne's driveway. "He wanted me to help pick out a Valentine's Day ring for

Mary Anne. Isn't that sweet? I can't go because of my new job. He's going to ask Kristy to go instead."

Robert reached out and took my hand. "I had fun tonight. Way to go on those strikes."

"You bowled strikes, Stacey?" Mom asked from the front seat.

"Two," Robert reported. "Thanks to Stacey we won one of the games. Logan and Mary Anne usually demolish us."

"Good work," said Mom. She dropped Robert at his house and I moved into the passenger seat beside her. "Did you have fun tonight?" she asked.

"Sure."

"I heard what you said about Logan buying a ring for Mary Anne," Mom said. "Does that mean they're going steady?"

"Mom, they already go steady," I said, just a little impatiently. "It's only, you know, a gift."

"When a boy gives a girl a ring it usually means something," said Mom.

"I don't think they're getting engaged or anything," I said.

Mom laughed. "No, they're a bit young for that."

"Yeah, just a bit. I wonder if they *will* wind up getting married. They're perfect together."

"A lot can go wrong between now and then," Mom said with a wistful sigh.

"I suppose," I agreed.

But I had no idea just how much was about to go wrong — and very soon!

CHAPTER 5

Monday came before I knew it. It was the day I started my job with the Cheplins. I made sure to wear my watch. The timing was going to be tight.

Robert met me at my locker as usual, when school let out. "Hi," I said as I gathered my books. "I can't talk. I have to run."

"Oh, your new job, right," he said. "Good luck."

"Thanks."

I hurried to the bike rack, hopped on my bike, and began riding as quickly as I could toward Acorn Place. I passed Claudia and Mary Anne walking together. "Remember, I'll be a little late today," I called to them.

They nodded and waved as I zoomed by.

At three-fifteen on the dot I skidded to a halt at the bus stop at the bottom of the hill. Barely a minute later, the bus chugged up the road and stopped. When the door opened,

Adam and Dana (whom I recognized from their photo), stood at the front of the bus staring at me. "I'm Stacey," I told the driver. "I'll be picking up Dana and Adam from now on."

"Oh, sure. Mrs. Cheplin mentioned it," replied the driver.

Adam smiled at me, but Dana eyed me suspiciously as they walked off the bus.

"Hi, how was school?" I asked cheerfully.

"It was really neat," Adam said enthusiastically in a lisping voice. "We went out and played a game, only Ralphie Meisner slipped on the ice and hit his head and he had to go to the nurse and I was his partner. I told Ralphie not to cry but he kept crying and crying. I let him blow his nose on my jacket sleeve because he already used his jacket and it was gross. Puuey! Yuck. Want to see my sleeve?" He held up his jacket sleeve and it certainly looked as if Ralphie had used it for a tissue.

"Ewww! That is so disgusting!" cried Dana. "Put your arm down. Get it away."

Adam shrugged and began walking up the hill. I walked beside Dana and Adam with my hands on my bike handlebars.

"How was *your* day, Dana?" I asked.

"All right, I suppose," she said in a ladylike manner. She adjusted the blue fleece headband she wore over her straight blonde bangs. "Can my friend Mandy come over?"

"I suppose so. If her mother says it's all right," I replied. "We can call when we get to the house."

"I know her phone number by heart," Dana told me. "Mandy and I are best friends."

At the house we called Mandy and I spoke to her mother. Mandy lived several houses away and would come over in a few minutes. The moment I hung up the phone, it rang again. It was Mrs. Cheplin. "Stacey, thank goodness," was how she greeted me. "Everything went all right?"

"No problem," I said. "We invited Mandy to play. Is that okay?"

"If you can handle an extra child, it's fine."

"I don't mind," I told her honestly.

"Great. Have Mandy go home by four-thirty so Dana can start her homework. I'd better go. See you at five-thirty."

" 'Bye."

On the kitchen table I saw a note written on a long yellow pad. *Dear Stacey*, it said. *Welcome to your first day of work. My office number is posted on the refrigerator. Here are a few things I need done today . . .* She wanted the laundry folded, the dishwasher unloaded and the dishes put away, and Adam's room tidied up.

I had brought along my Kid-Kit and a bag of art supplies for making valentines. I could see I wouldn't get the chance to use them, though. I'd have to work fast if I wanted to be available by four-thirty to help with homework. But I was pretty sure I could get it all done. I'd just have to stay organized.

"Anybody hungry?" I asked.

"I want peanut butter and jelly," Adam spoke up, pulling open the refrigerator. "That's what I always have. I like blueberry jelly a little, but I hate that black jelly with the seeds in it. Yuck! My most favorite is grape jelly but Mommy hates it and Dana can't have any so I eat all the grape jelly all by myself . . ." Adam just kept babbling on about jelly as he rummaged through the refrigerator.

"How about you?" I said to Dana. "Want some fruit or pretzels or something? Maybe a carrot stick?"

Dana studied me for a moment. "Do you know about my *disease*?" she asked.

"Your diabetes, yes," I replied. "You should eat a little something."

Dana lifted the corner of her lip in distaste. "All right. I'll have an apple, I guess."

I was about to tell her that I had diabetes, too, but just then the doorbell rang. Dana opened it to a girl with short brown hair and big brown eyes. "Hi, Mandy," she said. Mandy came in and looked at me. "This is Stacey," Dana told her, "my baby-sitter."

"Hi," said Mandy.

"Let's go play in the living room," Dana said to Mandy. "I want to play a board game. I know, we'll play Sorry."

"I can't open this!" Adam complained as he strained to twist the lid off of a peanut butter jar. I helped him open the jar and then made him a sandwich. While he ate it, I sliced two apples, put them on napkins, and brought each girl one in the living room where they were on the floor playing Sorry.

"Make sure you eat that," I told Dana. "It's important."

"I will," Dana agreed.

I went back to the narrow kitchen and unloaded the dishwasher while Adam ate. "Want to help me fold laundry?" I asked him when I was done with the dishes.

"No," he replied.

"Okay, but that's what I have to do next."

"I'll keep you company," he offered. "I'll play my Gameboy while you fold."

"Cool," I said, shutting the dishwasher. "Let's go."

I found the laundry basket near the washer and dryer, which were in a small washroom off a hall. I sat on a chair and folded. Adam sat on the floor beside me and turned on his Gameboy.

It wasn't hard to keep up a conversation with Adam because he did most of the talking.

He jumped from one topic to the other. He told me about his teacher, the kids in his class, and the play they were putting on in school. "I have a speaking part," he said. "Some kids are trees and they don't get to talk at all. I'm glad I get to talk."

I can imagine, I thought, trying hard not to laugh.

Just as I folded the last shirt, I heard the sound of angry voices coming from the living room. "I'd better go see what's going on," I told Adam as I tossed the folded undershirt into the basket.

As I drew closer to the living room I was able to hear what the girls were saying.

"We always do it your way!" Mandy said angrily.

"Do not!" Dana protested.

"We played what you wanted last time and the time before that," Mandy insisted.

"You're wrong," said Dana. "You wanted to play Clue last time and we did."

Mandy stood up. "That was your idea!"

"Was not!" Dana cried, throwing down a green peg from the Sorry game.

"Girls," I intervened. "What's the problem?"

"She wants to play a boring card game and I want to play Monopoly," Dana explained angrily.

"Go Fish is *not* a boring game," said Mandy, folding her arms stubbornly.

"Dana, I think you decided on the Sorry game you were just playing," I reminded her. "Why don't you let Mandy pick this game?"

Dana pressed her lips together and narrowed her eyes. I could see she wasn't happy with me. "Oh, all right," she mumbled.

Mandy sat down again. She reached out and plucked a box of playing cards from a bookshelf. "You can deal, Dana," she said, offering her the box. "Do you want to?"

Dana took the box and sullenly opened it, taking out the cards. I had just turned away from the girls, about to go back to Adam and the laundry, when Dana let out a low, pained groan.

"What's wrong?" I asked, turning back.

"I don't feel so good," she said in a trembling voice.

"What hurts?"

"I just feel all weak and shaky."

Weak and shaky? That's not a good sign coming from someone who's diabetic. My eyes darted to the napkins on the floor. Only one slice of apple remained. "Did you eat your apple?" I asked. I thought Mandy might have eaten both of them.

Dana nodded. "I ate the whole thing."

"Did you eat anything sweet today?" I

asked. "Mandy, you didn't bring over any candy, did you?"

Mandy shook her head. "Honest, I didn't. All we had were the apples."

Dana moaned again and held her head. I was beginning to feel worried. "Mandy, maybe you better go home," I said. "Dana should lie down."

"Okay," Mandy replied. " 'Bye, Dana. Hope you feel better."

Dana just grunted and nodded, looking too weak to reply. I hurried Mandy to the front hall and helped her into her coat. "Call when you get to your house," I told her, "so I know you got home safely."

"All right," Mandy agreed.

When I returned to the living room, Dana was lying on the floor with her eyes closed. Adam stood over her, gazing down, his large, brown eyes filled with concern. "I feel terrible," Dana said weakly.

I knelt and helped her to a sitting position. "Do you have a kit for testing your glucose?" I asked her.

"What?" Dana asked.

"Your blood sugar," I explained.

"Oh, yeah, that blood-taking thing. I have one on top of my dresser," she said. I left the kids and went upstairs. I had to find out if Dana's glucose levels were dangerously high or low. Even though she said she hadn't eaten sweets, she might be lying. After all, she was just a kid.

The second floor was smaller than the first. Two bedrooms and a bathroom nestled around a tiny, square hallway. One room was the kids' room. Inside the room, a thin, blue plywood wall separated Adam's space from Dana's. It was obviously one room that had been made into two. Adam's side was a clutter of toys, books, and clothing. Dana's side was neat, though, and it was easy to find her glucose test kit on top of her tall dresser.

I brought it back down to the living room. Dana was sitting up now with her chin propped on her knees. Adam sat beside her, his hand laid sympathetically on her knee. "Oh, not that thing, please," Dana whined when she spied the glucose kit. "I hate that!"

"It's not that bad," I said, kneeling beside her. "You get used to it."

"How would you know?" Dana asked disdainfully.

"Because I have diabetes, too."

Dana's eyes grew wide. "You do?"

"Uh-huh," I said, nodding. "I've done this test a zillion times. It's like nothing to me now. No big deal."

Dana scrunched her face and looked away as I pricked her finger with the needle-sharp point provided in the kit. She gasped as a tiny drop of red blood appeared on her finger. "Owwww. It hurts."

"Ew! Blood!" cried Adam, hopping around the room squeamishly.

While Dana sucked on her finger, I tested the blood sample with the kit. The digital number appeared on the read-out window. "Well, your blood sugar is within the normal range," I reported with relief.

"You mean my blood sugar is fine? You didn't even have to do that?" Dana asked, shaking her achy finger. "You pricked my finger for nothing?"

"I did have to," I said. "I had to know if your blood was all right. I would have had to get you to a doctor if it wasn't. If I hadn't done the test I wouldn't have known that you're okay."

Dana rolled forward into a floppy somersault. "Hey, Adam, bet you can't do this," she said, touching her nose with her tongue.

"Yes, I can." Adam took up the challenge. He stuck out his tongue but couldn't reach his nose.

"No, like this," Dana said, touching her nose with her tongue once again.

She seemed to have forgotten about feeling shaky.

"How do you feel?" I asked.

She raised her eyebrows thoughtfully. "Better. I think I feel better."

"Good," I said. "Come on, Adam, we have to straighten up your room." (Now that I'd had a glimpse of it, I realized I had to leave extra time to accomplish it.)

"I don't want to," Adam complained.

"If you don't tell me where everything should go I'll get all mixed up and you won't be able to find anything," I said.

Adam cocked his head. "That's true," he said with a giggle. "Okay."

"I'll help," Dana offered, getting to her feet.

"Do you feel well enough?" I asked.

"Yup."

We worked on Adam's room together and Dana seemed to have plenty of energy. Whatever had been bothering her had passed. By four-thirty, the cluttered room looked reasonably put together. "Time for homework," I told them.

We went downstairs to the living room. I sat on the couch and read *The Haunting of Grade One* with Adam, while Dana stretched out on the floor and did multiplication problems in her softcover math workbook.

At almost the stroke of five-thirty, Mrs. Cheplin walked into the house. She came into the living room just as I was checking Dana's final math problem. Adam was busily drawing a picture about the chapter we'd read together, which was his homework assignment.

The children jumped up to hug their mother. As she hugged them back she asked me how everything had gone.

"Fine," I said. "Dana wasn't feeling well so I tested her glucose level but it was normal. She feels okay now."

"That was very smart of you to check," Mrs. Cheplin said. She put her hand on Dana's forehead, checking for fever. "You look fine to me, kiddo," she said to her daughter.

"I feel fine," Dana told her.

"Diabetes can be tricky," I said.

"Were you able to get to the dishwasher and laundry?" she asked.

"Done," I reported.

"What about Adam's room?"

"It's much better than it was," I said.

"It looks excellent," Dana told her mother.

Mrs. Cheplin smiled. "I'm so pleased, Stacey. This is terrific."

"It wasn't really hard," I said. Except for the little scare with Dana, it hadn't been a problem.

Mrs. Cheplin paid me and I quickly said good-bye. I wanted to get to my BSC meeting by quarter to six if that was at all possible.

Outside, I grabbed my bike and started pedaling hard.

As I zoomed down the hill, my hair flying behind me, I felt pretty proud of myself. Stacey McGill, Super Sitter! That was me.

CHAPTER 6

Valentine's Day Tuesday fever
is in the air! When
I took Charlotte
Johanssen and Becca
downtown the other
day everyone
seemed to be out
shopping. And I do
mean everyone.
Becca and Char
sure got a case
of the giggles when
they saw a very
unlikely couple
buying a gift.

"**W**hat do you mean by an *unlikely* couple?" Mary Anne asked Jessi after reading Jessi's entry in the notebook. It was toward the end of our Wednesday meeting. (I'd just rushed in from the Cheplins' house.)

"Oh, just a couple," Jessi replied evasively. "You know, the kind of couple you wouldn't normally expect to find together."

Mary Anne scowled with confusion.

The rest of us looked at the floor or at the ceiling, trying not to laugh.

"What do you mean?" Mary Anne pressed. "Like he was tall and she was short, something like that?"

"Not exactly short and tall, but sort of like that," Jessi told her.

I, of course, knew what couple she was talking about. We all did, except Mary Anne. Jessi had told the rest of us who it was.

You see, when Jessi baby-sat for eight-year-old Charlotte Johanssen Tuesday afternoon, she brought her sister Becca with her. She also brought with her one of the valentine card craft kits Claudia had assembled.

"Cool! Wow! Cool!" Charlotte had gushed as Jessi spread the red paper, doilies, and foil out on the Johanssens' kitchen table.

But Becca frowned at the materials. "What's wrong?" Jessi asked.

"There's not enough stuff here to make really awesome valentines," she said.

"There's not?" Jessi asked.

"No," said Becca. "We need little flowers and stickers and stamps and maybe some glittery colored star stickers."

"You're right," Char agreed, propping her chin on her hands. "I want to make a super cool valentine for my parents."

Becca's eyes lit up with an idea. "Hey, could we go downtown to buy more supplies for our valentines? I have all my allowance money with me."

"I have money, too," said Char. "Please, let's go. Please! Please!"

It was cold out, but Jessi didn't really mind taking a walk downtown. "All right, I suppose so," she agreed. "Put your jackets on."

The girls pulled on their jackets, gloves, and hats in seconds. Soon they were all being blown down the street by a cold wind.

When they got downtown, they went straight to the stationery store. Char and Becca picked out glittery heart and star stickers, and split the cost of a cupid stamp and red inkpad. Jessi treated them to a roll of red satin ribbon from the gift wrap section.

They were on their way home when Becca suddenly stopped short in front of an accessories store called the Merry-Go-Round.

"What, Becca? What is it?" Jessi asked.

"Look inside there," Becca said, pointing through the glass door of the Merry-Go-Round. "It's Logan and he's with Kristy."

Char and Becca ran to the door. They put their hands on either side of their faces to help them see inside better.

Jessi looked over their heads into the store. Kristy and Logan stood at a jewelry counter. Jessi remembered my telling her that Kristy was helping Logan pick out a ring for Mary Anne, so she wasn't surprised when Logan turned and slipped a ring onto Kristy's finger.

"True love," Becca said in a silly voice.

Jessi playfully pushed Becca's woolen hat forward. "Come on, you two, let's get going." She rapped lightly on the door to get Logan's and Kristy's attention. When they looked up, she waved to them, then she steered Charlotte and Becca away from the door.

On the way home, the biting wind stung their faces. Jessi ducked her head to avoid it. As she walked she thought about Quint, a boy she knows who lives in New York City. He's also a ballet dancer so they have a lot in common. He studies at a very well-respected school called the Juilliard School, which is close to Lincoln Center, where many famous and wonderful ballets are performed.

Jessi couldn't decide whether to send Quint

a valentine. They write to one another sometimes, but a valentine is something different. They'd decided to just be friends, not boyfriend and girlfriend. Jessi didn't want to confuse things, yet she thought sending a valentine might be a nice, friendly thing to do.

Jessi thought about Quint and the possible valentine for an entire block. From there she started wondering what *kind* of valentine she should send if she decided to send one at all.

She was lost in these thoughts, and didn't notice Char and Becca giggling their heads off until they had nearly reached the Johanssens' house. "What's going on?" Jessi asked.

Char and Becca bit down on their giggles, but their eyes were still alive with mischievous fun. "What?" Jessi pressed. "What is it?"

"Oh, nothing," Char said in a singsong voice.

Jessi narrowed her eyes at them suspiciously.

Becca giggled. "Nothing at all," she echoed Char.

With that, the girls bolted into the house. Shaking her head, Jessi ran after them. They were already on the phone when she reached the kitchen, both of them giggling and whispering into the receiver.

"Who's on the phone?" Jessi demanded.

"Nobody," said Charlotte.

"Nobody?" Jessi asked incredulously.

"Not really." Charlotte giggled.

Becca cupped the mouthpiece of the phone. "Got to go," she whispered to the "nobody" at the other end. Quickly, she hung up.

Jessi's hands went to her hips. "Would you *please* tell me *what* is going on?" she asked with laughter in her voice. The girls were acting so silly it was hard not to laugh, but she was also becoming very curious about what they were up to.

Char shrugged with wide, outstretched arms. "Uh . . . you know . . . stuff."

"What kind of stuff?" Jessi asked.

"Valentines kind of stuff," Becca said.

"Speaking of that, want to start the valentines?" Jessi suggested as she pulled off her jacket and draped it over a kitchen chair.

"Okay," the girls agreed.

"Take off your jackets and let's start," said Jessi as she sat down at the table and began taking their new supplies out of the bag.

The girls pulled off their jackets and headed for the hallway to hang them up. While she waited, Jessi took the cellophane wrappers off the stickers and stamps and spread everything out on the table. She folded a piece of red paper and pondered what kind of valentine she should send to Quint, since by then she'd decided she *would* send him one. She decided a funny valentine would be best, but couldn't think of anything funny to say.

After a while Jessi realized that Becca and Charlotte hadn't returned from hanging up their coats. She went into the living room, but they weren't there, either.

Walking upstairs, she heard them giggling. She checked in Charlotte's bedroom. They weren't there.

Jessi followed the sound of the giggling to Dr. and Mr. Johanssen's room. The door was ajar and she could plainly see Char and Becca sitting on the Johanssens' bed, talking on the cordless phone they'd taken from the phone base on the night table.

The girls looked up and met Jessi's eyes.

"Oops." Charlotte laughed.

" 'Bye-'bye." Becca giggled into the phone.

"You two are acting so silly," said Jessi. *Who* are you calling?"

"Just some of our friends," Char said, scooting off the bed. "Can we make valentines now?"

"Of course," Jessi told her. "Come on downstairs."

Jessi told us that the girls were silly and giggly for the rest of the afternoon. Once they disappeared into the front hall closet together. When she opened it up they were sitting on the closet floor writing notes on memo pad paper. They wouldn't say what they were up to.

"It was the strangest afternoon," Jessi told us. "I was the only one who finished my valentine. Now I just have to decide whether to mail it."

CHAPTER 7

Let me tell you, my first week at the Cheplins' wasn't easy. Between school, baby-sitting, and my BSC meetings I felt as if I didn't have a moment to breathe. When I was at the Cheplins' there was no relaxing, either. Each day Mrs. Cheplin added one extra chore to her list. By Friday — the last day of my trial period — I was wondering if the list would ever stop growing.

That day it started snowing just as I picked Adam and Dana up from the bus stop. Adam danced around delightedly, sticking his tongue out to catch the flakes.

"There could be pollution in those flakes," Dana warned him as we walked up the hill.

"There is not," Adam said, examining the small crystals of snow on his glove.

When we reached the house I saw that Mrs. Cheplin's work list was the longest one yet. Fold the laundry, empty the dishwasher, tidy

Adam's room, throw wet wash into dryer, put stamps on envelopes in front hall and put out for mail carrier to pick up, put chopped meat from freezer into microwave to defrost, and empty wastebaskets into large plastic bag. All this had to be done before four-thirty, when homework was to start.

But, do you know what? I got it all done. Doing it made me feel sort of proud, too. So the chores were done by four-thirty and neither of the kids had homework over the weekend.

Finally a moment to breathe! That's what I thought.

"Can we play outside?" Adam asked.

"Please?" Dana seconded the idea. I didn't feel like going out, but how could I say no? It's not fair to keep kids in the house when it's snowing.

First, I made sure Dana had some carrot sticks for a snack. Then, we bundled up and went outside into the lightly falling snow, which fell in big fat flakes around us. In the last hour it had started to stick. There was almost an inch and a half on the ground.

We had only been outside for a minute when Mandy came along with a girl around Adam's age, maybe a little younger. "Hi, Moira!" Adam greeted the smaller girl as he ran to her.

At the same time, a boy and a girl Dana's age approached from the opposite direction. "Hi, Mandy. Hi, Dana," the girl called with a wave of her bright red mittens.

The boy waved, too, and soon the four of them were talking in the front yard while the two smaller kids chased one another in a circle off to the side of the house.

They didn't seem to need me for entertainment. I stood for a moment and enjoyed the beauty of the falling snow. Then I spied a snow shovel leaning against the house.

The snow must have put me in a good mood. Or maybe it was just the fact that it was Friday. But I decided it would be nice for Mrs. Cheplin to come home to a shoveled walk and driveway. (Or maybe I was just showing off a bit. You know, being Stacey McGill, Super Sitter.)

I was shoveling away when the first snowball flew past me. "Sorry!" Mandy called from the yard when I looked around to see what was happening. Mandy and the two other kids were having fun throwing snowballs at one another. The only one who wasn't smiling was Dana, who stood frowning, her arms folded.

"Let's do something else," I heard her say. "Let's build a snowman."

"No, let's have snowball teams," the boy said. "You and Mandy against Ellen and me."

"Yeah! Come on, Dana," said Mandy. "We can get them good."

I checked on Adam and Moira, then went back to my shoveling. The snow was falling so fast now that the walk was filling in almost as fast as I could shovel it out. Oh, well, I thought. This makes it a little easier for Mrs. Cheplin to shovel.

I'd shoveled almost to the front door when I noticed Dana coming toward me looking very unhappy. "What's wrong?" I asked.

"I don't feel good," she replied. "I'm weak and sort of dizzy."

"Did you cheat on sweets today?" I asked. She shook her head.

"You have to tell me the truth," I insisted. "It's really important. No kidding."

"I didn't. Honest."

"I'd better check your blood again to be safe," I said, resting my shovel against the house. I turned toward Adam and told him not to leave the yard.

"We'll watch him," Mandy called to me.

Dana and I went inside and tested her blood. "Normal," I reported. I felt her forehead. "No fever, either."

Dana slumped onto the living room loveseat. "I don't want to play outside anymore," she mumbled. "I want to rest."

"You *should* rest," I agreed.

I called Adam in. I didn't want to leave him out there unsupervised for too long. With a long, disappointed face, he said good-bye to Moira and joined me at the front door.

Moira ran to Mandy, who had waited in the yard. "Is Dana all right?" Mandy asked, coming toward me.

"I'm not sure. I think she should rest, though," I replied.

"We should have built a snowman like she wanted," Mandy said apologetically. "I keep forgetting how sick she is."

"Don't worry. You didn't do anything wrong," I assured her. As I spoke the words, I began to wonder about something. Was Dana using her diabetes as a means of getting her own way? Were the guilty feelings Mandy was experiencing exactly the feelings Dana wanted her to have? I remembered how instantly Dana had recovered on Monday once the argument was over. Would the same thing happen today?

"Tell Dana I hope she feels better," Mandy said as she and Moira left the yard.

Just as I suspected, when Adam and I went back inside Dana looked a *lot* better. In fact within half an hour she wanted us to watch her do a cartwheel she'd learned that day in gym class.

I wondered if I should talk to Mrs. Cheplin

about what I thought Dana was up to. It was a bad direction for her to be going in. Not only was it unfair to her friends, but it was bad for Dana. If she believed she could manipulate people, she might use her illness as an excuse to duck out on anything challenging.

Truthfully, though, I couldn't picture myself having that conversation with Mrs. Cheplin. We'd just met and, so far, I didn't feel all that comfortable around her. Every evening she came home and looked around the house as if she were *sure* I'd messed up in some way. I could tell she didn't completely trust me yet.

Instead, I decided to drop a big hint directly to Dana. When Adam went to his room to get a book I saw my chance to talk alone with Dana.

"Wow!" I said, sitting next to Dana on the living room floor. "This has been some busy week for me. I didn't think I could get everything done that I had to do, but I did it."

"That's good," she said as she got to her knees and switched on the TV.

"I used to worry that my diabetes would stop me from doing things I wanted to do, but it hasn't. This busy week sure proves that."

Dana studied me. "Don't you get more tired than other kids?" she asked.

"Not if I take care of myself." I checked the clock on the wall. It was five-twenty. "Gee, I hope this snow doesn't make your mother late getting home. I have to go to my Baby-sitters Club meeting. Kristy, our president, gets really annoyed if we're late. Of course, I've been coming late because I'm sitting with you and Adam, but I can tell Kristy isn't happy with it. The sooner I get there the better."

"She sounds mean," Dana said.

"Oh, no, she's not."

"She should understand that you're sick and you shouldn't be rushing around."

I looked Dana squarely in the face to be sure she'd understand what I was about to tell her. "I wouldn't want to be treated differently from everyone else because I'm sick."

"Why not?"

I had to think about that for a moment. "Because it wouldn't be fair to ask for special treatment."

"Why not? You're sick."

"But the kind of sickness we have doesn't stop us from doing anything so it's not fair to ask to be treated differently."

Dana didn't look pleased. She turned away from me and started watching TV. I wondered if anything I said would make a difference. Somehow, I didn't think so.

Adam came into the room and wanted me to read a book called *Backward Bunny* to him. It was a short book and just as I was finishing,

Mrs. Cheplin came in, stomping snow from her boots. "Thanks for shoveling, Stacey," she said. "I can see you made a path."

"You're welcome," I replied.

Adam jumped up to greet his mother. "Mom! Mom! We played in the snow. It was great. I played with Moira. But Dana spoiled it with her sickness."

Alarm spread across Mrs. Cheplin's face. "Dana's sick?"

"She seems fine now. And her blood sugar is okay. I tested it," I told her.

Mrs. Cheplin scowled. "I'd better call Doctor Hernandez. This is worrying me."

This was my chance to say something, but I just couldn't.

As usual, Mrs. Cheplin checked around to see if everything had been done. And — as usual — she found that everything had been done. "A beautiful job, Stacey," she said.

"Thanks," I replied as I gathered my things. I wasn't looking forward to riding my bike to Claudia's in the snow.

"I'd say you've done a wonderful job this week," said Mrs. Cheplin. "How would you like to extend the job for two more weeks?"

I didn't understand. If I'd done such a great job why was she offering me just two more weeks?

She must have sensed my confusion because

she explained, "At the end of the two weeks if things are still this great, we'll make a permanent arrangement."

"All right," I said, but I wasn't happy. This long probation didn't seem fair.

"I'll expect a bit more work done in the next two weeks," she said.

More work! Was she kidding? There was no way I could do more work.

"Mrs. Cheplin," I began, "I don't think that — "

"Naturally I'll pay you more for the additional housework," she cut in. Then she told me how *much* more. "What were you about to say, Stacey?"

"I don't think that will be a problem," I replied. At this rate, I'd have enough money for my theater tickets at the end of the two weeks and maybe even enough to take Robert to dinner if we didn't go anywhere too fancy.

"We'll see how we both feel it's going at the end of two weeks," Mrs. Cheplin said as she took money from her wallet and paid me.

"Sounds great," I told her, taking the money and heading for the door. "Have a nice weekend. See you Monday."

"Wait, Stacey. Let me drive you home," said Mrs. Cheplin. "We can put your bike in the trunk."

She bundled up the kids and we drove to

Claudia's house through the falling snow.

Despite the bad road conditions, I got to the meeting sooner than usual. "How's the job going?" Kristy asked me.

"Great," I said. "I mean . . . there are some annoying things about it . . . but the money is great. Yeah . . . it's great."

CHAPTER 8

Greed. It's a dangerous thing.

That's what I was thinking the following Wednesday as I ran around the Cheplins' house like a maniac trying to accomplish Mrs. Cheplin's ever growing list of things to be done.

How I'd come to dread that list. I even had nightmares about it. The night before I'd dreamt that I was walking home from school with Robert, and Mrs. Cheplin walked right behind us telling me all the things she wanted done in a steady stream of chatter. And, in my dream, her chores were even worse than in real life. "Stacey, paint the house, wash the windows, patch all the clothes, do the grocery shopping, fix the roof, cook a lasagna." In the dream I covered my ears and tried to get away from her but she chased me, rambling on about her list all the while. "Wallpaper the living room, carpet the stairs, get rid of my clutter, cure Dana's diabetes.''

That's when I woke up. "I can't!" I cried, still half in my dream. Then I woke up fully and realized I was in my bedroom. I was glad to be out of *that* dream.

But I wanted the money. Was that greed? In a way, it was. Because now I no longer wanted only to take Robert to Broadway. Now I also wanted to take him somewhere fancy for dinner. I also wanted to buy a new dress, something that would look special for this special night.

I'd also started thinking about other ways I could spend the money if I continued working for Mrs. Cheplin. My biggest plan was to save for a sports car. After all, I'd be old enough to drive in a few years. That was enough time to save a good-sized down payment on a car. I spent a lot of time imagining myself cruising to Manhattan in a hot red convertible.

In order for these plans to come true, I needed to keep my high-paying job with Mrs. Cheplin. That meant making sure everything on her list was accomplished.

Unfortunately, the real list was only slightly better than the one in my nightmares. So far on that Wednesday I'd already given the kids snacks, straightened up Adam's room, and unloaded the dishwasher. A plumber arrived to fix a leak under the sink. (Mrs. Cheplin had told me the day before that he was coming.) He spread his tools and piping out all over the tiny kitchen floor and crawled under the sink to check things out.

Now I had to take Dana to her first piano lesson at a house at the top of the hill. Of course, I had to bring Adam with me, too. Just bundling him up in boots, snowsuit, scarf, and hat was a job.

We trudged up Acorn Place to the home of a woman who gave piano lessons. "I don't think I want to go," Dana announced when we reached the front door. "And I don't feel so good all of a sudden."

I took a deep breath. By now I was sure this was a gimmick of Dana's to get out of doing certain things. "Just go in and check it out," I told her. "Adam and I will be right outside."

"I really feel sick," she insisted.

I put my hand between her shoulder blades and gently guided her toward the front door. "I think your mother has already paid for these lessons. She really wants you to go." As I spoke, I rang the doorbell. A friendly-looking lady with short white hair came to the door. "Hello, Mrs. Kleinsasser," I said. "Dana's here for her lesson."

"Come in, Dana." Mrs. Kleinsasser greeted

her warmly. With slumped shoulders, Dana went inside.

Adam and I built a snowman on the side of Mrs. Kleinsasser's house while we waited for Dana. Chatterbox Adam told me all about his parents' divorce. "My daddy got a job in Chicago and he wanted to go and my mommy didn't want to go and they had a big fight. So then he went but we stayed here. Daddy calls us every night and he's going to visit us in the spring. We're going to live with him this summer."

"This summer?" I gasped. That meant I wouldn't be earning this money through the summer. I'd have to take that into account when I was calculating things.

"Yes, we'll be with him all summer. He lives in an apartment building with a pool and . . ."

I didn't listen to the rest of what he had to say. I was busy adding up what I *wouldn't* be making this summer and subtracting it from the total yearly amount that I'd calculated days ago.

At the end of the hour, Dana came outside smiling. "It was great," she reported.

"How do you feel?" I asked.

"Fine," she said.

I wasn't surprised.

I hurried the kids back down the hill as fast

as Adam's short legs would go. I knew I'd lost a precious hour waiting at the Kleinsassers' and would have to make up some time. When we reached the house, the plumber was still under the sink.

I checked the list. Stamp outgoing bills. Make dentist appointment for Adam. Fold laundry.

When those things were done, "peel carrots" was next on my list. "It's homework time," Adam said as I stepped over a box of plumbers' tools to reach a pack of carrots in the refrigerator. Checking the wall clock, I saw that he was right. I'd never get everything done in time!

Think, Stacey, think, I urged myself. There had to be a way. "I'll peel while you read," I suggested.

We sat at the kitchen table. I peeled while Adam read me *Martin and the Tooth Fairy.*

After awhile, Dana came to the table holding her math workbook. "Stacey, I don't understand this."

"Let me see," I said.

"Hey, I'm reading!" Adam cried indignantly.

"I can still listen."

"No, you can't," he protested.

"Dana, just wait till he stops reading."

"Look at how much he has left," Dana said.

"And he reads so slow." She was right. He did have a long way to go.

"Adam, keep reading. Really, I can listen."

"Oh, all right," said Adam.

Still peeling carrots into a brown paper bag, I looked at Dana's division problem and tried to keep part of my mind on Adam's reading.

"Young lady," the plumber called from near the front door. "I turned off the water. I'm going out to check one of the pipes that runs outside."

"Okay," I called over my shoulder.

I had just turned back to Dana's division problem when my hand slipped and I scraped my thumb on the peeler. "Ow!" I cried, jumping to my feet, waving my throbbing hand in the air.

Adam burst into tears.

"What's wrong?" I asked as I tried to shake the pain from my hand.

"You're not listening to me read!" he cried, tears sliding down his cheeks.

"Oh, stop it, you big baby!" Dana scolded him.

Mrs. Cheplin picked that moment to walk in the front door. "What's going on here?" she asked.

Adam ran to his mother and threw his tearful face into her side. "Stacey won't listen to me read!" he sobbed.

Mrs. Cheplin looked at me with questioning eyes. "I *was* listening, but . . ." I began. My voice trailed off because Mrs. Cheplin *wasn't* listening. She was looking around the kitchen.

"This place is a mess!" she cried, glaring at me accusingly. "What's all this?"

"The plumber," I reminded her.

"Where is he?" Mrs. Cheplin asked.

"Outside. He's checking something."

With troubled eyes, Mrs. Cheplin continued looking around the house, checking to see if everything was done. I had the strangest feeling that Mrs. Cheplin almost hoped to find something not done. "Did Dana go to her piano lesson?" she asked me.

"Yes."

"You didn't start the rice," she said, sounding displeased.

It was the last thing on the list and it was true, I hadn't gotten to it. Then I thought fast. "The plumber turned the water off." Even if I'd wanted to start the rice I wouldn't have been able to boil the water for it.

Looking at me suspiciously, Mrs. Cheplin went to the sink and turned the faucet. Water spurted out.

"Honest," I said. "That's what he told me."

Mrs. Cheplin rolled her eyes and wiped some black gook from the kitchen counter. The plumber had left it there, but Mrs. Cheplin looked at me as if I should have cleaned up after him already.

I felt really angry. Why was I knocking myself out to please this woman who didn't appreciate what I did and only looked to find fault? Who did she think she was, anyway? I opened my mouth to tell her what I thought when the plumber came in the front door.

He nodded at Mrs. Cheplin. "One of your outside lines was frozen so the water couldn't pass. It backed up and that's what caused the leak in your system. I torched the frozen clog free, which might send some water through your line, but to keep a continuous flow I have to turn the water back on. Once I do that you'll be fine."

"Wonderful," Mrs. Cheplin told the plumber. "I see you were right about the water," she said to me. "You couldn't have started the rice."

No, I thought bitterly. You'll have to make it yourself. What a horror. You'll actually have to boil a pot of water.

Plumber or no plumber, if Dana was going to go to piano lessons I wouldn't be able to get so many things done on those days. Mrs. Cheplin would just have to understand that. I took a deep breath, preparing to tell her that, when Mrs. Cheplin handed me my pay.

I looked down at the money in my hand. A

picture of Robert and me in New York flashed through my mind. Another image — me in my flashy red car — whizzed across my brain, too.

I folded the money and stuffed it into the back pocket of my jeans. "Thanks," I said. "See you tomorrow."

As I said, greed is a dangerous thing.

CHAPTER 9

Wednesday

Kristy and I had the weirdest day baby-sitting at my house. I know sitting with my brothers and sisters is always a little crazy, but this time they weren't the problem.

Some kids are really mad at me. But who are they? They don't want me to know. I'm making it my business to find out, though.

While I was at the Cheplins' struggling with plumbers and piano lessons, Mallory and Kristy were having a hard time of their own. They were at Mal's sitting for the younger Pikes. Mrs. Pike always hires two sitters since there are so many kids.

Byron, Jordan, and Adam Pike were making a snow fort in the yard. They'd decided this was going to be the snow fort to end all snow forts. They kept thinking of great additions to their fort and running in and out of the house for the supplies they needed.

"You're tracking mushy snow all over the kitchen floor!" Mallory scolded Byron. She was sitting at the table helping Vanessa and Margo cut out red construction paper valentines to make a valentine chain.

"Stop bugging me, Mallory." Byron blew her off as he opened the cabinet that held the pots and pans. He rummaged through it until he pulled out a metal strainer. "Just what I need," he announced triumphantly.

"What are you going to use that for?" asked Kristy as she walked into the kitchen with Claire. Claire had chocolate smeared all over her face and Kristy was looking for a cloth to clean her up with.

"We're going to shoot water through the strainer so it will spray all over the place and

90

create a wall of ice over our fort."

"Byron, you'll get wet and freeze out there," Kristy protested as she wiped Claire's face.

"Besides, Dad shut the outside faucets off for the winter," Mallory added.

Just then, something crashed in the living room. Kristy and Mallory ran to see what had happened.

Nicky lay by a bookcase with a heap of Mr. Pike's books lying around him. "Are you all right?" cried Kristy, helping Nicky to his feet.

"What were you doing?" Mal asked.

"Nothing," said Nicky, rubbing his knee.

Mallory reached under the couch and pulled out a skateboard. "Is this the nothing you were doing?" she asked.

"Sort of," Nicky admitted. There was a two-foot edge of wood floor around the living room rug that Nicky had been trying (unsuccessfully) to navigate.

Just then, the phone in the kitchen rang. "I'll get it," said Kristy, heading into the kitchen. "Pike residence," she said as she picked up the receiver.

"Is this Crusty?" asked a kid's voice.

"Do you mean Kristy?"

"No Crusty. Crusty Toenails. That's you!" Click. The kid on the other end hung up.

Shaking her head, Kristy hung up. Was that call meant for her, or would the caller have asked for Crusty Toenails no matter who picked up?

"Who was that?" Mal asked, rejoining Margo, Vanessa, and Claire at the kitchen table.

"Just a prank call," Kristy reported.

At that moment, the front doorbell rang. "I'll get it," said Kristy. When she opened the door, no one was there. "Hello?" she called out. She checked to see if anyone was hiding in the bushes. No one was there.

When she returned to the kitchen, the triplets were raiding the refrigerator looking for treats to load into the snow chest they'd built inside their fort. "You can't take all that stuff outside," Mallory told them as they grabbed ice cream from the freezer and cupcakes from the top of the refrigerator.

"Yeah, like we're really scared of you, Mallory," Adam said as he filled his arms with containers of juice and chocolate milk from the refrigerator.

Mallory looked to Kristy for help.

"Drop it, you guys," Kristy commanded. Then she gave them the Look.

Without another word, the triplets began putting back the food.

The front door bell rang again. Kristy sighed in exasperation. "I'll get it."

This time, she went to the window first and

peeked through the curtains. She didn't see anyone, but the bushes beneath the window were shaking as if someone were moving below them. Kristy sprang to the door and pulled it open.

Looking sharply to the right, she saw a kid's jeans and boots disappear around the corner of the house. She tore out of the doorway and ran to the side of the house. Whoever had been there was fast because he'd completely disappeared.

It wasn't until Kristy returned to the front door that she noticed the envelope taped to it. On the front was written *Crusty*.

Kristy opened the envelope as she entered the house. She took out a piece of paper and saw written on it in a child's handwriting:

Crusty is a girl we know
she looks like Pinocchio
When she comes down the street
you can smell her dirty feet.
When she runs around the house
she looks like a scrawny mouse.
Crusty's clothes are never clean
she's ugly and she's really mean.

"What's that?" Mallory asked, looking over Kristy's shoulder.

"Just some hate mail from a few of my fans," Kristy replied wryly.

"How dumb," Mal commented as she read the note. "Vanessa!" she cried.

Vanessa came in from the kitchen. "What's the matter?"

"You like to write poetry," Mal said, showing her the note. "What do you know about this?"

Vanessa read the note then looked up with wide, innocent eyes. "I didn't write this," she said.

"Do you know who did?" Mallory asked.

"I never saw it before in my life." Vanessa turned and hurried upstairs.

Kristy and Mal looked at one another. "That may be so," said Mal, "but she didn't say she doesn't know who wrote it." Mallory headed for the stairs. "I'll get to the bottom of this," she said.

"Don't bother," said Kristy. "It's just kids being dumb. I wonder if it has anything to do with Kristy's Krushers? I sometimes get this kind of stuff when the Krushers win a lot of games in a row. The Bashers get angry. You know, sore losers. But it's winter. The season hasn't even started."

The phone rang again. This time Mal picked it up, but all she heard was a click as someone on the other end hung up.

By the time Mrs. Pike returned at five, the doorbell had rung two more times, and Kristy had found an unflattering picture of herself drawn in crayon shoved under the front door. Also, someone on the phone had muttered, "Beware, you are headed for doom, Crusty."

"What's going on?" Mal asked as they headed to Claudia's house.

"I have *no* idea," said Kristy. And for Kristy, that was a first.

CHAPTER 10

"Well, you're turning into your father's daughter," Mom said to me on Saturday morning as she came into my bedroom and opened the curtains, letting in a flood of sunshine.

I peeked out from under my covers. I couldn't believe how tired I was even though I'd slept eight hours. At least I thought I'd slept eight hours until I glanced at the clock on the stand beside my bed. It was ten o'clock. I'd slept twelve hours! I *never* do that!

Rubbing my eyes, I sat up in bed. "What do you mean, my father's daughter?" I asked Mom. What was she talking about?

"You're becoming a workaholic just like your father."

"Huh? Why did you say that?"

Mom turned to me and smiled, but her smile seemed forced. "Well, in the morning, you're up and running to school. Then you race to the Cheplins'. Three days a week you hurry from there to your club meetings. You gulp down dinner so you can get to your homework. When you finish it, you're so exhausted you fall into bed. Just like your father."

I knew what she meant. My dad would leave for work early, come home late, and even work on weekends.

Tossing off the covers, I swung my legs to the floor. "But I'm making so much money," I told Mom.

A breathy, surprised laugh escaped Mom's lips. "That's *exactly* what your father says."

"Maybe we *are* alike," I said. Mom and I had always agreed that Dad's being a working maniac was a giant pain for us. But I had never understood how it felt from his point of view. Now I did. When you have an opportunity to make money you take it. And making money can be exciting. All of a sudden, you can think about having and doing all sorts of things that once seemed out of reach. (My red convertible sports car, for example.)

Mom suddenly looked sad. I realized she hadn't expected me to admit I might be like Dad. "I might be like him but I'm not a workaholic," I said, hoping to make her feel better. "I'm not working this weekend."

"Good," Mom said with a genuine smile.

Of course, I could very well have been working that weekend if a job had come up at a BSC meeting. Luckily, though, the others were interested in the weekend jobs so they didn't need me to take any of them.

"I know," Mom said brightly. "Since I've barely seen you these last few weeks, why don't we do something together this afternoon? We could go see a really, really sad movie. I'm in the mood to sit and cry into a large popcorn."

"You are?" I said, concerned.

Mom grinned sheepishly. "I am," she admitted. "Nothing's wrong, just a mood. There's nothing like a good movie-generated cry once in awhile."

"Sorry," I said. "I have an English paper due on Monday and I have to finish up my research today because the library's closed tomorrow."

"What about going tonight?" she suggested.

I grimaced. "I made plans to go out with Robert tonight. I haven't seen much of him lately, either."

I could see the disappointment in Mom's eyes. "All right," she said.

"Want to go tomorrow?" I asked.

"I don't know. I could really use that cry today. Maybe I'll go to the movies by myself."

As she left the room I knew I'd seen that look on her face before. The last time I'd seen it was when Mom and Dad were still married and he told us we'd have to take our vacation on Martha's Vineyard without him because he suddenly had to give a huge presentation to the board members of his company.

What else could I do, though? The paper had to get done. I was sure Mom wouldn't want me to let my schoolwork slide just to go to the movies with her. I'd thought I could get it done during the week, but by the time I finished my homework each night I was too tired to start researching the life of F. Scott Fitzgerald, which was the topic of my paper.

I decided Mom would feel better after she had her good cry.

And I'd feel better after that paper was out of the way. I dressed in jeans and a thick red sweater, tied my hair back in a red scrunchy, and headed downstairs. After a quick breakfast I grabbed my backpack and my jacket and hurried to the Stoneybrook library.

Mrs. Kishi, Claudia's mother, is the head librarian. "Hi, Stacey," she greeted me as I flipped through the F section of the card catalogue.

"Hi, Mrs. Kishi," I replied. "What's Claudia up to today?"

Mrs. Kishi shifted the armful of books she was carrying onto the top of a low cabinet. "Nothing much. I think she's working on an outfit to wear tomorrow."

"What's happening tomorrow?" I asked.

"Aren't you two going to the Valentine's Day Craft Fair at the community center?"

My hand flew to my mouth. Claudia and I had made plans weeks ago to go to the fair. "That's right! I forgot about it completely," I admitted.

Mrs. Kishi replaced the stack of books one by one onto the shelf. "I think Claudia's working on an outfit and making up business cards to give out to people at the fair who might be interested in having similar outfits made up for Valentine's Day."

I now remembered Claudia mentioning this plan to me. She hoped people would comment on her customized sweat outfit decorated with lace and satin hearts, and order some for Valentine's Day or other occasions. She figured she could make some easy and fun money that way.

I'd been so busy with the Cheplins it had completely slipped my mind. I was glad Mrs. Kishi had reminded me.

I said good-bye to her and gathered up my research books on Fitzgerald. There was a lot more to know about him than I realized. This paper counted for a fourth of my grade this term, too. It was supposed to be well-researched with footnotes and a bibliography.

I threw myself into the project. I barely lifted my head until a few hours later when I sensed someone staring at me. I looked up into Robert's eyes. "Hi," I said, smiling. "How did you find me?"

"Your mother told me you were here," he said as he took a seat beside me. "How's the work coming?"

"Not good," I said with a frown. "I haven't even begun writing this thing yet. I'm hours away from starting to write and it's due Monday." I looked at him and sighed. "Robert, would you hate me forever if we don't go out tonight?"

"Why not?" he asked unhappily.

"Because I'll never get this thing done otherwise."

"Do it Sunday."

"Can't," I told him. "I promised Claudia I'd go to this crafts fair with her."

"Cancel that, then," said Robert.

"Robert, I made the plans with her weeks

ago. I just can't cancel them now."

"Then how come you can cancel your plans with me?"

"Well . . ." I said in a quavery voice. "I made my plans with you *after* I made the plans with Claudia. At the time I thought I could do both, but I can't."

"Stacey, I've hardly seen you at all in the last few weeks," Robert pointed out, getting to his feet.

I wanted to tell him that one of the reasons I was so busy was because I was earning money for *his* birthday present. That would have spoiled the surprise, though, so I kept quiet. "I *promise* we'll do something next weekend," I said.

"All right." He forced a smile. "I'll leave so you can finish your paper." He turned and left without looking back at me once. I felt terrible.

Once he was gone, I stared at the library door, thinking about Robert. Then I told myself to get back to work.

I read about Fitzgerald and took notes until the library closed at six o'clock. When I got home, Mom was making dinner. "Did you finish your paper?" she asked.

"Not yet," I reported as I gulped down my chicken. After dinner I hurried to my room to begin writing my paper from the notes I'd put on index cards at the library. The work went more slowly than I expected. Somehow the words just didn't flow out of me. I don't know, maybe I was too tired to think straight. Normally, I would have let the work go until Sunday, but I wouldn't be free on Sunday.

It was sometime in the middle of the night when I fell asleep on my bed with my research material spread out around me. Mom must have come in during the night because in the morning I awoke, still fully dressed, but under my covers with my index cards, books, and notebook neatly stacked on my night table.

I'd barely opened my eyes when Mom came into my room. "Claudia's waiting for you downstairs," she said. "Were you supposed to go to a crafts fair with her today?"

"What time is it?" I cried, bolting out of bed. It was after noon. Still half asleep, I charged out of my room and down the stairs.

Claudia was at the bottom of the stairs. "What happened to you?" she gasped.

I realized I probably looked like a crazy person with my rumpled clothes, sleepy face, and tangled hair. "I overslept," I admitted. "Can you wait a few minutes?"

Claudia glanced toward the door. "My father's waiting in the car, but I guess so. Hurry up, though."

I staggered a few steps up the stairs, then stopped short.

"What's wrong?" Claud asked.

"My paper," I said. "It's still not written." I turned and faced her. "But that's okay," I said, backing up the stairs, "Don't worry. I can do it tonight."

"Do you have much more to write?" Claudia asked.

"You could say that."

"How much more?"

"Half."

"You'd better just stay home," Claudia said. "You're not in any shape to go out."

"Yes, I am. I am," I assured her. "Just give me a minute."

"Stacey!"

"What!"

"I'm leaving without you. You're a wreck. Go back to sleep."

"I'm fine! Just wait for me."

" 'Bye," Claudia said, waving to me from the bottom of the stairs. "See you tomorrow. Get some rest."

I watched with mixed emotions as she went out the door. I felt bad about letting her down.

But I was *not* in the mood to go and I was glad to be let off the hook.

With sleepy eyes, I stumbled back to my room. And fell face first onto my bed. In an instant I was sound asleep.

CHAPTER 11

The next day, I was still thinking about F. Scott Fitzgerald as I waited for Adam and Dana's bus to arrive. I'd handed in my paper, but I had no idea whether or not it was any good. I'd been so sleepy while writing it that I could barely remember what I'd written.

The bus pulled to a stop and I met Dana and Adam. As usual, Adam talked in a steady stream as we climbed the hill. Dana was unusually quiet, though. "Is something wrong?" I asked her while I unlocked the front door.

"No," she said with a shrug.

"Do you feel all right?"

She nodded dully. "Yup."

We walked into the house and I picked up Mrs. Cheplin's note. "I don't believe this," I muttered. It was two pages long.

"Okay, kids," I said, shrugging off my jacket. "I'll fix you a snack, then you have to go play until homework time. I have a lot to do today." As quickly as I could, I smeared peanut butter on some crackers for Adam and tossed an apple to Dana.

The kids took their snacks upstairs and I honestly didn't know *what* they were doing for the next hour as I swept the kitchen floor, unloaded the dishwasher, sorted a load of dirty laundry, shifted a load of wet clothes from the washing machine into the dryer, and put another load into the washing machine. Then I called to cancel Mrs. Cheplin's subscription to a magazine, confirmed Adam's dentist appointment, and called to find rates on the gymnastics lessons he wanted to take.

I was in the middle of peeling potatoes for dinner (the third to last item on my list) when Dana came into the kitchen. "I don't feel so good," she said.

I continued peeling potatoes over the sink. *What doesn't she want to do this time?* I wondered. "I don't have the time for this, Dana," I said with an edge in my voice.

"Fine!" Dana whirled around and stomped out of the kitchen.

Instant remorse. I shouldn't have been so crabby with her. Wiping my hands on a kitchen towel, I left the kitchen and found Dana lying on the loveseat in the living room.

"Sorry, Dana," I said. "What hurts?"

"Forget it," Dana mumbled. "Don't bother."

"Come on, Dana," I pleaded. "I said I was sorry." I noticed that Dana *did* look pale. I remembered how listless she'd seemed on the way home. "I'm going to get your kit and test your blood," I told her.

"Nooooo," Dana whined. "I hate that! I hate it! I'm not doing it!" She rolled over and buried her face into the back of the loveseat.

Upstairs, I found the glucose testing kit on top of Dana's dresser. "Dana's being a big crab," Adam called to me from his room.

"I know, but she's not feeling well," I told him. A glance into his room made me cringe. Over the weekend he'd managed to undo two week's worth of daily tidying (which was the second to last thing on my list that day). "Adam, start cleaning your room, okay?" I said.

"I'll wait for you," he replied. Oh, well, I hadn't really expected that to work, anyway.

"Get away from me with that!" Dana shouted when I returned to the living room. She'd never reacted this badly to having her blood tested. Her sudden unreasonableness worried me. Irritability can be a sign that a person's blood sugar is low.

"Dana," I said sternly. "I'm going to test

your blood so you might as well cooperate and we can get it over with quickly."

Dana covered her face with a pillow and shot her free arm out at me. I took firm hold of her finger, pricked it, and wiped away my tiny blood sample.

In less than a minute I had a reading.

Dana's blood sugar was dangerously low.

A wave of panic swept over me. What should I do? Calm down, I ordered myself. Think!

Running to the kitchen, I flung open the refrigerator and grabbed an orange. I peeled it as I walked back to the living room, letting the peels drop on the floor. "Eat this," I ordered, handing Dana the orange.

Dana ate the orange, but five minutes later she looked just as listless as before. I had to do something quickly.

I ran back to the refrigerator and found the name and phone number of Dana's doctor. An answering machine picked up and said the doctor was on vacation. What could I do now?

"Dr. Johanssen," I said aloud. I could take Dana to her house. I knew she was home on Monday afternoons. Just then, the phone rang. I snapped it up, hoping it would be Mrs. Cheplin. "Hello?"

It was Mrs. Kleinsasser calling to reschedule Dana's piano lesson. I was desperate. "Could you drive us somewhere?" I blurted out. "I need to get to a doctor." I explained what was going on and Mrs. Kleinsasser said she'd be right over.

When I returned to the living room, Dana looked even paler. I could see the delicate blue veins at the sides of her temples. She had curled up on the loveseat and closed her eyes. "Come on," I said. "Get up. We're going to see a doctor."

The fight seemed to have gone out of Dana. Limply she let me help her on with her jacket. "Adam!" I called. "Adam, come down here."

Outside, a car horn honked. Looking out the window, I saw Mrs. Kleinsasser sitting behind the wheel of her blue compact station wagon. "Hurry, Adam!" I yelled, then ran up the stairs to get him.

When Adam was downstairs, I tossed his jacket over his shoulders and hurried the two kids out the door.

Mrs. Kleinsasser drove us to Dr. Johanssen's house. "Do you think we should go to the hospital instead?" she asked.

"Let's try Dr. Johanssen first," I suggested.

Charlotte answered the door when we arrived. "Mom!" she called. Dr. Johanssen hurried out of the kitchen. I introduced Mrs. Kleinsasser, then explained Dana's problem.

"Let's have a look at you," Dr. Johanssen told Dana, gently guiding her toward her study.

Char showed us her new video game while Mrs. Kleinsasser, Adam, and I waited in the living room. In half an hour, Dana and Dr. Johanssen returned. The color had come back to Dana's cheeks and she looked a whole lot better.

"She'll be all right now," said Dr. Johanssen. "Stacey, please tell Mrs. Cheplin to call me when she gets in. Dana's insulin dosage will probably have to be adjusted. I'm going to call her doctor, Dr. Hernandez, and leave a message for him to call me as soon as he returns."

"Thanks a million, Dr. Johanssen," I said, feeling incredibly relieved.

"You're welcome. You did the right thing to bring her here, Stacey," Dr. Johanssen told me.

"Thanks."

We rode home and Mrs. Kleinsasser dropped us off outside the house. "Would you like me to come in?" she offered.

"No, I see Mrs. Cheplin's car in the driveway," I said. "Thank you very much."

When we entered the house, Mrs. Cheplin came out of the kitchen to meet us. She was red-faced with anger. "*What* happened here today?" she barked at me. I opened my mouth to tell her but she obviously didn't want an answer.

"When I came home the door was unlocked. Look at this place! Potato peelings all over the table. Adam's room is a wreck! Supper isn't even started!"

"Mrs. Cheplin, we had an — " I began.

"I don't care what you had! There is no excuse for this! I knew you were too young to handle this job. I should have listened to my instincts. They told me to hire an older girl. Nonetheless, I can't believe you would — "

"Mrs. Cheplin!" I said, raising my voice. "Would you please listen!"

She widened her eyes, but she didn't say anything.

"I had to rush out because Dana's blood sugar was too low. I asked Mrs. Kleinsasser to drive her to my friend Dr. Johanssen's house."

Mrs. Cheplin turned pale. "Dana, how do you feel?"

"Fine now," Dana answered.

"Did you have a snack when you came home?"

"She had an orange and an apple," I said. "Dr. Johanssen wants you to call her. She thinks Dana's insulin dosage might need to be changed. I have her number." As I spoke, I wrote down the number (which I knew by heart since I baby-sit for Char a lot) on the memo pad in the front hallway.

"Stacey, I'm sorry," said Mrs. Cheplin. "I had no idea."

I was too angry to accept her apology. How dare she speak to me like that after I'd worked like crazy to comply with her stupid list *and* taken good care of her kids at the same time. I was furious.

"I'm late for my meeting," I said, gathering my books. " 'Bye."

CHAPTER 12

TUESDAY

SOMETIMES THE ADORABLE LITTLE
KIDS WE SIT FOR CAN REALLY BE
ANNOYING — ESPECIALLY MY SISTER
KERRY. I AM STEAMING. SHE AND
HER PALS HAVE COMPLETELY RUINED
MY VALENTINE'S DAY PLANS WITH
MARY ANNE.

It rained all day Tuesday, washing away the last of the snow. Logan was home baby-sitting for his five-year-old brother Hunter, and his ten-year-old sister, Kerry.

"I knew something was up with Kerry when I found her sitting in the linen closet whispering into the cordless phone," he told us at Wednesday's meeting. (He decided to attend the meeting since he was walking Mary Anne over to Claudia's anyway.)

"What's with the kids and the secret phone calls lately?" Kristy wondered aloud.

"We found out," Mary Anne told her. "And wait until you hear."

"You won't believe it," Logan added.

Logan told us he wasn't paying too much attention at first to Kerry and her mysterious phone calls. He figured she was just being silly with her friends. He sat down with Hunter at the family's new computer to fool around with a CD-Rom program they'd just bought.

He was busily zooming around a "virtual" road when the doorbell rang. Logan handed Hunter the computer mouse and ran to the door.

Opening the door, Logan looked out on the rainy day but didn't see anyone. Then, he glanced down and saw a soggy envelope struck under the doormat.

Logan was pretty sure he knew what it was. This wasn't the first time that week that an envelope had been delivered by some ring-and-run phantom. Here's what the letter said.

Logan is no friend of mine.
He looks just like Frankenstein.
When he comes down the street,
you can smell his dirty feet.
Logan is a dirty bum and he is
a great big crumb.

Crumpling the note, he tossed it into the wastebasket and returned to Hunter at the computer. "Who was it?" Hunter asked as his "virtual" sportscar crashed into a "virtual" brick wall.

"Just some idiot playing a joke," Logan said lightly, taking back the mouse.

"Huh?"

"Never mind." Logan laughed. "What's the score?"

While Logan continued playing, he wondered about the letters he'd been receiving. Who was sending them? And why? He had no idea. He tried to remember if he'd made any kids mad while baby-sitting, but he hadn't even been sitting much lately.

About five minutes later, the doorbell rang again. This time Logan was in no mood to get up and answer it. (Besides, he was in the process of beating his previous score.) "Kerry!" he bellowed. "Kerry, get the door!"

Kerry popped up from behind the living room sofa still clutching the cordless phone. "You don't have to shout," she said huffily. "I'm going."

When Kerry didn't return in nearly five minutes, Logan assumed one of her friends had been at the door. But then the responsible sitter in him surfaced and he decided he'd better check on her. "Take over for me," he told Hunter as he handed him the mouse once again.

"Is this my score now?" Hunter asked enthusiastically.

Logan hesitated for a moment. "Uh . . . yeah . . . sure. It's yours."

Just as he stood up, Kerry came into the room. "There are some people outside to see you," she said in a strangely superior tone.

"What people?" Logan asked, frowning.

"People who have something to say to you."

Logan shot Kerry a confused, questioning look and headed for the front door. When he opened it, he came face-to-face with ten of the kids we baby-sit for, and they were all scowling furiously at him. (Even Dana Cheplin was there. Apparently she's a friend of Vanessa's.)

"What's up, guys?" Logan asked.

"That's what we came to ask *you*!" said Vanessa dramatically.

"What are you talking about?" Logan asked.

"Oh, sure, like you don't know," Haley Braddock scoffed.

Claire Pike stepped forward, her arms folded tightly. "You two-dimer!" she scolded.

"What?" asked Logan.

"That's two-*timer*," Nicky corrected his sister.

"Two-timer?" Logan echoed in bewilderment.

Just then, Mary Anne came up the walk. Logan was glad to see her. Maybe she knew what was going on.

"What's all this?" Mary Anne asked when she reached the front door.

"I was hoping you knew," Logan said.

Jenny Prezzioso and Margo Pike ran to Mary Anne and put their arms around her. "Poor Mary Anne," said Jenny.

"Poor, sweet, trusting Mary Anne," Margo agreed, gazing up at Mary Anne with wide, pity-filled eyes.

Logan and Mary Anne exchanged glances of complete bewilderment. *What* was going on?

Haley stepped up to Mary Anne and took her hand. "Logan has a confession to make.

It won't be easy for you, but you have all of us to lean on."

"Th-thanks," Mary Anne said.

"What confession?" Logan yelped indignantly.

"A confession about the ring you gave to *another woman!*" Kerry cried accusingly.

At that point, Mary Anne became just a little alarmed. "What is she talking about, Logan?" she asked.

Logan was laughing too hard to reply.

"He thinks this is funny!" Vanessa cried, outraged.

"It is funny," Logan sputtered through his laughter. "It's very funny."

"It is?" Mary Anne said. "Maybe someone better tell me what's going on."

"Logan has lost his mind," Haley said. "That's what's going on."

"Just great!" exclaimed Kerry, throwing up her arms in exasperation. "First he acts like a rat, then he covers up by acting insane."

"I'm not a rat and I'm not insane. This is all a big mistake."

"You can't get out of it," Becca said. "Vanessa and I saw you buy that ring for Kristy!"

"You bought Kristy a ring?" Mary Anne gasped.

"Oops," said Becca, covering her mouth.

Apparently she hadn't meant for that to slip out then.

"Mary Anne, I bought the ring for you," Logan explained patiently. "Kristy was helping me pick it out. It was supposed to be a Valentine's Day surprise."

"Oh, Logan, thank you," Mary Anne said, growing misty-eyed.

"You're welcome, but thanks to these guys the surprise is ruined." Logan gave the kids an annoyed stare. "Luckily I have one more valentine surprise lined up."

Kerry cleared her throat uncomfortably. Her face was red around the temples and chin. "Uh . . . no you don't," she said in a small voice.

Logan looked at her sharply.

"I . . . uh . . . I . . . uh," Kerry stammered.

"You what?" Logan demanded.

"I kind of canceled your reservation at Chez Maurice," Kerry said quickly.

"You're taking me to Chez Maurice!" Mary Anne cried.

"Not anymore," said Logan. "I won't be able to get another reservation there this close to Valentine's Day." He turned angrily toward his sister. "Kerry, I'm going to brain you! Why did you do that?"

"I heard you make the reservation. Becca had called to tell me about you and Kristy.

So I put two and two together and — "

"And you got six," Logan filled in for her.

"Well, we thought you were being untrue to Mary Anne," Vanessa said defensively.

Mary Anne took Logan's hand. "Logan would never do something like that," she told the kids. "But I do appreciate your sticking up for me. That was very sweet." She turned to Logan. "You have to admit, it *was* sweet."

Logan just scowled.

"Sorry, Logan," said Buddy Barrett. One by one the kids apologized as they turned and slunk away from the front door.

"At least that solves the hate-mail mystery," Mary Anne said with a rueful laugh.

Logan nodded. "It sure does. Now the mystery is what we are going to do to celebrate Valentine's Day."

CHAPTER 13

When I reached the Cheplins' on Thursday I was happy to see that Mrs. Cheplin had scaled her chore list back to one page. Maybe that was her way of making up for being so obnoxious before. I was especially glad because I was hoping to find a little extra time to make a valentine card for Robert.

I'd been so crazed lately that I hadn't gotten anything for him. If I hadn't heard Logan's story at the Wednesday meeting I might have forgotten about Valentine's Day altogether.

I was racing through my first chore, unloading the dishwasher, when Dana came into the kitchen wearing her jacket. "Adam and I are going over to Kerry Bruno's house," she announced.

"Sorry, but I don't think so," I told her. "Are you allowed to walk down the hill alone? There aren't any sidewalks."

"No, but Kerry really needs us and I said

we would come," Dana pleaded.

"Needs you for what?"

"For the Valentine's Day dinner," she told me. "It's to make up to Mary Anne and Logan for the trouble we caused."

"Oh," I said thoughtfully. That was awfully sweet of them. I hated to say no. But I had so many chores to do!

"I'll walk you down there," I said finally. "We can't stay long, though."

"Yea!" Dana cheered.

So I bundled up the kids and walked down the hill and over to Logan's house, which is on Burnt Hill Road. When we rang the bell, Kerry was thrilled to see me. "Excellent!" she cried, pulling me in the door. "We desperately need someone who can cook."

The kitchen reminded me of Santa's workshop on Christmas Eve. Except that the elves were our baby-sitting charges and instead of making toys, they were preparing food.

At the kitchen table, Vanessa and Becca were cutting out Jell-O hearts with cookie cutters. Nicky Pike decorated them with swirls of canned whipped cream. Margo was creating a fruit punch from many jars and cans of juice. Haley was using a plastic knife to slice bananas and toss them into the punch. Matt Braddock was assembling dishes to set the table.

Kerry presented me with an opened pack of

chopped meat, which already had hunks gouged out of it. "I tried to make hamburgers in the microwave but they came out gross," she said, wrinkling her nose.

"Super gross," Jenny confirmed as she took bread from the breadbox on the counter.

I thought a moment and remembered that meat didn't brown in a microwave. "You need to use the stove top," I told her. "I can do it for you."

I found some onions and chopped them quickly. I let them fry while I made the hamburger patties, seasoning them with salt, pepper, and some dried garlic.

At four o'clock the doorbell rang. A buzz of excitement swept through the group. "Mary Anne is here," Kerry told me. "We invited her to come at four."

Everyone scurried to put the last touches on their projects. Vanessa slipped into a tuxedo jacket she'd found in the family costume box. She draped a white towel over her bent arm. "I'm going out," she announced. "This is it. Everybody get ready."

We gathered at the open kitchen doorway as Vanessa strutted out to the living room where Mary Anne and Logan stood talking. "Where's Kerry?" Logan asked Vanessa. "Do you know why she told Mary Anne to come over here right away?" He sounded angry. He probably thought this was another scheme the kids had concocted. (He was right about *that*, only this was a good scheme.)

"As a matter of fact, I do," said Vanessa. "Follow me, if you please."

"Now what?" Logan sighed as he and Mary Anne followed Vanessa toward the dining room. The rest of us jumped back out of the kitchen doorway as they approached so we wouldn't spoil the surprise.

Vanessa stopped just outside the doorway. "Your table is ready," she said with a low bow.

"Oh, wow!" Mary Anne cried when she spied the beautifully set table with red construction paper placements and paper doily napkins. A big red tissue paper flower sat in a glass in the middle of the table.

Vanessa pulled out a chair and Mary Anne sat down.

With a nudge, Haley pushed her brother Matt out of the kitchen. He was holding a water pitcher. He filled Logan's and Mary Anne's glasses, splashing some over the side. "No problem," Logan said, mopping up the spill with his doily napkin.

I dashed back to the stove and put a hamburger and some onions on two plates. Becca took one and Margo took the other out to the table. Haley trailed behind them, struggling to keep hold of the pitcher of fruit punch with floating bananas.

As soon as Logan and Mary Anne picked up their forks to eat, the kids ran out to sing the romantic serenade they'd practiced. First they sang a song from *Lady and the Tramp*.

Peeking out of the kitchen, I could see that Logan was working hard not to laugh. Mary Anne was trying equally hard not to cry. I noticed a delicate ring on her finger.

The kids then went into a pretty awful rendition of "Can You Feel the Love (Tonight)?" Then they backed out of the room.

As Adam and Dana returned to the kitchen, I grabbed their coats. "We've *got* to go," I told them. "I have so much to do before your mother gets home."

"Please can we stay?" Dana pleaded. "We haven't served dessert yet."

Just then, Mary Anne stuck her head in the kitchen door. "Could we have two more napkins, please?" she requested.

"Coming up!" Kerry said, scrambling to grab some paper napkins.

"Please, can't we stay?" Dana begged.

"Homework," I reminded her.

"I only have fifteen minutes of homework

and I'll read with Adam. I promise."

"I could walk them home," Mary Anne offered.

I considered this. I'd get more done without the kids. And Mary Anne didn't live far away. "They have to be home by five," I told her. "Five-fifteen at the latest."

"All right," Mary Anne agreed.

"Thanks," I said, grabbing my parka. I dashed out of the house and began hurrying back to the Cheplins' house. Why was I so desperate to complete Mrs. Cheplin's stupid list? I wondered as I chugged up the hill as fast as I could go.

Was it just greed? Maybe. But somehow I felt something more was involved. I think I wanted to prove to Mrs. Cheplin that I could do the job simply because she thought I couldn't.

Besides, she was paying me to do a job, so I wanted to do it as well as I possibly could. But was Mrs. Cheplin being unreasonable? I decided she was. She might even have been taking advantage of me because I'm young. Or maybe she somehow sensed I was someone who would try to do my best no matter what she asked.

As I unlocked the door, I realized I was angry. Why should I knock myself out for this

woman who didn't appreciate anything anyway?

After that, I didn't have time to think about
my anger. I was too busy flying around the
house trying to finish everything.

CHAPTER 14

Instead of feeling like Stacey McGill, Super Sitter, I felt as if my new nickname should be Barely-Made-It-McGill.

That Thursday — which was Valentine's Day — I barely made it through Mrs. Cheplin's chores. Mary Anne returned the kids about three seconds before Mrs. Cheplin arrived. I had to admit that the kids hadn't done their homework, which didn't make Mrs. Cheplin too happy.

From there, I pedaled home like a maniac so I could rework my paper on F. Scott Fitzgerald. (My teacher said it felt "a little rushed." Ha! If only she knew! She very kindly gave me a chance to do it over.)

Believe me, it's hard to make a paper seem not rushed when you're rushing through it. Which is exactly what I was doing when the doorbell rang.

"Stacey!" Mom called up the stairs. "It's Robert."

I jumped up from my desk. "Robert!" I gasped. I'd completely forgotten to make him a Valentine's Day card! How could I have forgotten?

"Maybe he forgot, too," I said aloud as I leaped up from my bed. He hadn't given me anything in school that day.

I considered claiming to feel sick and not going downstairs. No, that was a bit *too* infantile. (I'd been hanging around with Dana Cheplin too long.) I really had no choice but to pray that Robert hadn't brought me anything for Valentine's Day.

I walked down the stairs, trying to look calm and happy to see Robert.

Robert stood at the bottom of the stairs. As I've said, each time I see him I swear he's cuter than he was before. "Hi," I said, smiling. "I didn't know you were coming over."

"It's Valentine's Day," he said. That's when I realized he was holding one hand behind his back. That could mean only one thing.

"Here," he said when I reached the bottom of the stairs. "This is for you."

In his hand he held one long-stemmed red rose and a small box wrapped in red wrapping tissue. "Thank you," I said as I took the rose and smelled it. Laying the rose down on a side

130

table, I unwrapped the box. "Wow!" I gasped when I opened it. Inside was a gorgeous gold necklace with a delicate prism looped onto it. "It's gorgeous," I said sincerely, putting it on. "I love it!"

"Do you really?" Robert asked.

"Yes, really!"

Slowly, my smile faded. It was the moment of truth. "I don't have anything for you," I said apologetically.

I studied Robert, but it was hard to read his expression. He blinked as if he were absorbing this news and trying to figure out how he felt about it. "That's okay," he said.

"No, it's not." I took his hand. "I'm so sorry. Really. I am. I meant to at least make you a card, but then everything got so crazy today at the Cheplins'."

"It sounds like things are always crazy over there."

"I know, but today I had to take the kids to Logan's. You know, I told you how the kids canceled Logan's reservation so they tried to make it up to them by making them a valentine's dinner and — "

Robert held up his hand to stop me. "I want to hear about it, but later. It's nice that they had a valentine's dinner, but what about us? You seemed so touched that Logan was buying Mary Anne a ring. That made me think

Valentine's Day must be important to you. Is it?"

"It is, Robert," I wailed. How had I let things get so out of hand? "It's really important. And so are you. I know it must not look that way right now. This job at the Cheplins' is making me nuts. My whole life is falling apart!"

"Stacey, I think Mrs. Cheplin is taking advantage of you."

"You do?" I said. "You know, I've been feeling the same way." I sighed. "I might as well tell you why I took the job to begin with."

"Why?"

"I wanted money for your birthday present," I admitted. "I took the job because of you, but because of the job I've hurt your feelings."

"My feelings aren't hurt," Robert said. "What's my present?"

"I'm not telling. But it's something I hope will make you like New York City better."

"Oh, Stacey," he said, taking my other hand in his. "Do you mean you've been doing all this just because I said I didn't like the city?"

I nodded.

"I'll give the city a try if it's that important to you," Robert said softly.

"You will?" I asked, looking up.

"Sure." Gently he pulled me closer and we

kissed. I was so lucky to have Robert.

I stepped back and stood a moment, staring into Robert's eyes.

I jumped when my mother walked into the hall. She jumped, too. "Oh, sorry," she said, embarrassed.

"I have to go," Robert said awkwardly. "I'll see you in school tomorrow, Stace."

" 'Bye, Robert," I said dreamily. "Thanks for the necklace and the rose."

"You're welcome. 'Bye."

Robert left and Mom picked up the rose from the sidetable. "How sweet," she said wistfully. "Let me see the necklace."

I showed it to her and she sighed. "I remember when I used to get gifts on Valentine's Day."

I put my hand on her shoulder, seeing for the first time how lonely she must be feeling. I'd been so absorbed in my hectic schedule I hadn't thought about her much. But I saw now how she missed me, and how she missed having someone special to spend Valentine's Day with.

"*An Affair to Remember* is on," Mom said.

"What's that?" I asked.

"It's a great old movie. It stars Cary Grant. It's wonderfully sad."

"You nuke the popcorn, I'll get the tissues," I suggested.

"Really?" Mom said with a surprised smile.

"Sure. I wouldn't mind a good cry either." I picked up the remote control and snapped on the TV. F. Scott Fitzgerald would just have to wait.

CHAPTER 15

I handed in old F. Scott first thing Friday morning, although I don't think this paper was any less rushed than the one before it. I'd gotten up at five-thirty in the morning to finish typing it. (After *An Affair to Remember* I'd wiped my eyes and barely had enough energy left to stumble up the stairs to bed.)

As I sat in English class that morning my eyes felt dry and sandy, my throat was scratchy, and my brain was definitely foggy. Face it — I was a mess.

I hated feeling this way. At least it was the last day of the week. I just had to pray that Kristy didn't guilt me into taking any job that came up at the meeting that afternoon. I wanted to be free to sleep all weekend.

Wait a minute! I thought, my eyes opening wide for the first time all morning. I couldn't sleep all weekend. I was supposed to go to my father's.

Usually I look forward to seeing Dad, but I was so exhausted that I didn't even want to go. Maybe I could cancel. But, no. Dad was looking forward to seeing me. If I canceled, especially this late, it would ruin his weekend. I'd be letting him down, just like I'd let down Robert.

So I had to go, although I wouldn't be very good company. I hoped Dad hadn't bought the tickets to that show. I'd probably fall asleep in the middle of the play.

Tired as I was, I somehow made it through the day. The bus was waiting when I reached Dana's and Adam's stop. Thankfully the bus driver waited a moment for me to arrive.

"You look terrible," said Dana as she got off the bus.

I could imagine. At lunchtime I had circles under my eyes and red splotches on my cheeks. I probably looked even worse now.

When I saw Mrs. Cheplin's list I nearly burst into tears. It was two pages long again.

"Could we play a game today?" Adam asked.

"Sorry, Adam," I said. "I have too much to do."

"You always have too much to do."

"I know, I know," I muttered as I headed for the kitchen.

That day the chores were torture. Not only was I exhausted, but midway through the chores I realized I was angry. I resented having to do so much housework. I didn't think it was fair to Adam and Dana, either. I couldn't spend any time with them at all.

I finished the last chore just as Mrs. Cheplin walked in the door. The kids had been great. They'd done their homework without any help from me. (I had no idea whether they needed help or not.)

Barely-Made-It McGill slides through once again, I thought, blowing a stray piece of hair from my face.

"You've done very well this week, Stacey," said Mrs. Cheplin, looking around as she always did.

"Thanks," I said without enthusiasm. To tell you the truth, I wanted to tell her off. Or maybe just to step on her toe very hard. I took my money and got ready to leave.

"Stacey, I'm so pleased with your work. I'd like to offer you another two-week job."

"Another two weeks?" I repeated dully. Suddenly I saw what was going on. Mrs. Cheplin was going to keep me on probation forever. I'd have to prove myself endlessly.

"I don't know," I told her.

"I'll pay you twice as much," she said.

Twice as much? I could take Robert to the best play in town. I'd have my sports car in half the time. Perhaps I could buy it without even getting a loan.

"Can I call you tonight?" I asked. "I need to think about it."

Mrs. Cheplin's face fell. "Is something wrong, Stacey?" The tables had turned. Now *she* was concerned about pleasing me.

"I just need to think about a few things," I told her.

I said good-bye to Dana and Adam and rode my bike toward Claudia's house. When I arrived I threw myself onto her bed. "What's wrong?" asked Kristy, alarmed.

Everyone gathered around me. "Are you okay?" asked Mallory.

"No," I said, tears brimming in my eyes. "I'm not okay." I poured out the whole story — everything, how I'd been feeling, how I ruined Valentine's Day, how I'd deserted my mom and had no energy for my father this weekend. "And I'm sure I'm going to get a terrible grade on my English paper even after I got a second chance at it. Now Mrs. Cheplin just offered me twice as much money to stay on, and I can't say no to it."

"Why not?" Claudia asked.

"What do you mean why not? I need the money. You know that."

"Do you need it more than friends and family and good grades in school?" Kristy asked.

"No," I admitted.

"You don't need it more than your health," said Claudia. "You don't look so good."

"I know." I wiped the tears from my eyes. "And I don't need it more than my brain. I feel like that's the next thing to go."

"Quit," Kristy said simply.

"Mrs. Cheplin sounds like a pain, anyway," Abby added.

"She is a pain. But I don't want to leave her stranded."

"She'll find someone else," Jessi said. "She might need a grown person who has a car and no homework at the end of the day."

"She might," I said. "But she won't find someone quickly."

"Tell her one of us will come over every day until she finds someone permanent," Kristy suggested. "But we don't do housework."

"Okay," I said. "I will."

As the meeting wore on, I realized I was feeling better and better. I had needed the support of my friends to help me make the decision to quit, but I'd made it.

I called Mrs. Cheplin as soon as I got home.

"This is Stacey," I said. "I've decided not to take your offer for the next two weeks."

At first there was silence at the other end of the phone. "Why not?" she asked after a moment.

"Mrs. Cheplin, I feel taken advantage of," I said. "The lists of chores are way too long. I don't think it's good for the kids when the person taking care of them is tied up with housework. They need attention, too."

I decided not to add my complaints about her attitude or the way she wouldn't commit to a steady job. I'd said enough already. I'd said the important things.

I suppose I'd hoped she'd say, "Oh, Stacey, you're right. I've been so wrong. I'm sorry."

That's not what she said.

"Obviously, you don't have the maturity required for this job," was her reply.

"No, I don't have the *time*," I said politely. I told her she could count on the BSC for fill-in sitters until she found someone permanent. "Tell the kids I'll miss them."

"They'll miss you, too," she said grudgingly. "Good-bye."

" 'Bye."

I hung up the phone and drew in a deep breath. Then I jumped up and punched the air. "Yes!" I shouted. I was free. I could have a normal life again. There was no doubt in my mind that I'd done the right thing. It felt right. And I was glad I'd mentioned the housework problem. Dana and Adam needed attention more than they needed a tidy house.

Mom came into the kitchen. "What happened?" she asked.

"I've just learned a big lesson about what's important in life and what's not," I told her.

"You have?" she asked, looking pleased.

"Yes. I was allowing money to be the most important thing in my life. My job at the Cheplin's was taking over everything."

"It was?"

"Yeah. Like friendship and you and Robert. My schoolwork was suffering. And the worst part was that I didn't even have time for me. I didn't have a minute to think a thought or to relax."

Mom smiled. "You *have* learned a lot. I'm glad."

I phoned Robert and told him the good news. He was very glad to hear it. "Way to go!" he cried. "That took guts, Stace. I'm proud of you."

He couldn't have said anything nicer.

"This weekend I'm going to buy those tickets and then Dad and I are going to have a long talk," I said to Mom that evening as we prepared supper together.

"About what?" she asked.

"About *not* being a father–daughter team of workaholics! There's so much more to life!"

Dear Reader:

Over the years I've heard from lots of BSC fans — both through the mail and on-line — about problems they've had with their own baby-sitting jobs. Many kids have asked for advice about what to do when they're expected to perform household chores in addition to sitting, and they're being paid only for sitting. That sparked the idea for *Stacey McGill, Super Sitter*. In Stacey's case, she knew what she was getting into, but her job quickly got out of hand!

Remember that any time you're baby-sitting, you are responsible for leaving the house as neat as it was when you arrived. If you've fed the kids a meal, make sure you clean the kitchen afterward; if the kids have done a messy art project, make sure you tidy up after them. But if you're asked to do extra chores or errands, you should be paid for it. Talk things over ahead of time with the client. One other tip for you super sitters — don't be afraid to talk about problems with your clients. They'll appreciate your honesty, and recognize you as a responsible sitter.

Happy reading and happy sitting,

Ann M. Martin

Ann M. Martin

About the Author

ANN MATTHEWS MARTIN was born on August 12, 1955. She grew up in Princeton, NJ, with her parents and her younger sister, Jane.

Although Ann used to be a teacher and then an editor of children's books, she's now a full-time writer. She gets the ideas for her books from many different places. Some are based on personal experiences. Others are based on childhood memories and feelings. Many are written about contemporary problems or events.

All of Ann's characters, even the members of the Baby-sitters Club, are made up. (So is Stoneybrook.) But many of her characters are based on real people. Sometimes Ann names her characters after people she knows, other times she chooses names she likes.

In addition to the Baby-sitters Club books, Ann Martin has written many other books for children. Her favorite is *Ten Kids, No Pets* because she loves big families and she loves animals. Her favorite Baby-sitters Club book is *Kristy's Big Day*. (By the way, Kristy is her favorite baby-sitter!)

Ann M. Martin now lives in New York with her cats, Gussie and Woody. Her hobbies are reading, sewing, and needlework — especially making clothes for children.

Notebook Pages

This Baby-sitters Club book belongs to _____.

I am _____ years old and in the _____

grade.

The name of my school is _____.

I got this BSC book from _____.

I started reading it on _____ and

finished reading it on _____.

The place where I read most of this book is _____.

My favorite part was when _____.

If I could change anything in the story, it might be the part when

_____.

My favorite character in the Baby-sitters Club is _____.

The BSC member I am most like is _____

because _____.

If I could write a Baby-sitters Club book it would be about ___

_____.

#94 Stacey McGill, Super Sitter

As a Super Sitter, Stacey does many chores for Mrs. Cheplin in addition to baby-sitting, including sweeping, dusting, and peeling potatoes. Some of the chores I have to do are

_____ .

The chore I hate the most is _____ .

One chore that I don't mind doing is _____ .

Some of the things that I buy with my chore and/or sitting money

are: _____

_____ . Right now, I am saving money or want to save

money so I can _____

_____ . Stacey saves up her sitting money to buy

dinner and tickets to a Broadway show for a special evening with

Robert. If I could take anyone for a special night out, it would

be _____ .

Some of the things I would do with this person are: _____

_____ . If I could go

anywhere in the world on a date, I would go to _____

_____ with _____ .

STACEY'S

Here I am, age three.

Me with Charlot
my "almos

A family portrait — me
with my parents.

SCRAPBOOK

ohanssen,
ister."

Getting ready for school.

In LUV at Shadow Lake.

Illustrations by Angelo Tillery

Read all the books
about **Stacey**
in the Baby-sitters Club series
by Ann M. Martin

Look for #95

KRISTY + BART = ?

Bart bought the popcorn — no butter, lots of salt — and two sodas, and we walked into the theater. Bart began edging into the third-to-the-back row.

"Too far," I said. "Let's go closer."

Bart was already plopping himself into a seat. "I bought the popcorn," he said with a grin, "so I get to choose where we sit."

"Maybe we can rent binoculars," I remarked.

But I sat. As the lights dimmed, I reached for the popcorn.

Bart put his arm around the back of my seat. "Is it salty enough?" he asked.

"Fome," I replied. (I was trying to say *fine*, but my mouth was full.)

Bart's arm landed on my shoulder as the previews came on.

The movie's opening scene was so exciting.

I forgot about my appetite. It quickly spun into a complicated plot about an international smuggling ring. A car chase, a disappearing motorboat, a footrace over some city rooftops — I loved it.

Eventually the movie bogged down in the love scene, when the male and female leads do just what everyone has expected them to do. I start snoozing.

I could feel my eyelids growing heavier. On-screen, an actor playing a spy was looking all gooey-eyed at an undercover policewoman. His big face looked closer . . . closer . . . so close you could see his skin pores . . .

I felt something warm on my left cheek.

I jerked away. Bart was inches away, leaning over my seat.

He laughed. I laughed. I settled back into my seat.

And then Bart kissed me.

THE BABY-SITTERS CLUB®

The best friends you'll ever have!

Collect 'em all!

by Ann M. Martin

More titles... ▶

☐ MG48222-X	#78	**Claudia and the Crazy Peaches**	$3.50
☐ MG48223-8	#79	**Mary Anne Breaks the Rules**	$3.50
☐ MG48224-6	#80	**Mallory Pike, #1 Fan**	$3.50
☐ MG48225-4	#81	**Kristy and Mr. Mom**	$3.50
☐ MG48226-2	#82	**Jessi and the Troublemaker**	$3.50
☐ MG48235-1	#83	**Stacey vs. the BSC**	$3.50
☐ MG48228-9	#84	**Dawn and the School Spirit War**	$3.50
☐ MG48236-X	#85	**Claudi Kishli, Live from WSTO**	$3.50
☐ MG48227-0	#86	**Mary Anne and Camp BSC**	$3.50
☐ MG48237-8	#87	**Stacey and the Bad Girls**	$3.50
☐ MG22872-2	#88	**Farewell, Dawn**	$3.50
☐ MG22873-0	#89	**Kristy and the Dirty Diapers**	$3.50
☐ MG22874-9	#90	**Welcome to the BSC, Abby**	$3.50
☐ MG22875-1	#91	**Claudia and the First Thanksgiving**	$3.50
☐ MG22876-5	#92	**Mallory's Christmas Wish**	$3.50
☐ MG22877-3	#93	**Mary Anne and the Memory Garden**	$3.99
☐ MG22878-1	#94	**Stacey McGill, Super Sitter**	$3.99
☐ MG45575-3		**Logan's Story Special Edition Readers' Request**	$3.25
☐ MG47118-X		**Logan Bruno, Boy Baby-sitter** **Special Edition Readers' Request**	$3.50
☐ MG47756-0		**Shannon's Story Special Edition**	$3.50
☐ MG47686-6		**The Baby-sitters Club Guide to Baby-sitting**	$3.25
☐ MG47314-X		**The Baby-sitters Club Trivia and Puzzle Fun Book**	$2.50
☐ MG48400-1		**BSC Portrait Collection: Claudia's Book**	$3.50
☐ MG22864-1		**BSC Portrait Collection: Dawn's Book**	$3.50
☐ MG48399-4		**BSC Portrait Collection: Stacey's Book**	$3.50
☐ MG47151-1		**The Baby-sitters Club Chain Letter**	$14.95
☐ MG48295-5		**The Baby-sitters Club Secret Santa**	$14.95
☐ MG45074-3		**The Baby-sitters Club Notebook**	$2.50
☐ MG44783-1		**The Baby-sitters Club Postcard Book**	$4.95

Available wherever you buy books...or use this order form.

Scholastic Inc., P.O. Box 7502, 2931 E. McCarty Street, Jefferson City, MO 65102

Please send me the books I have checked above. I am enclosing $_____
(please add $2.00 to cover shipping and handling). Send check or money order–no cash or
C.O.D.s please.

Name _____ Birthdate_____

Address _____

City_____ State/Zip _____
Please allow four to six weeks for delivery. Offer good in the U.S. only. Sorry, mail orders are not available
to residents of Canada. Prices subject to change.

THE BABY-SITTERS CLUB

by Ann M. Martin

Collect and read these exciting BSC Super Specials, Mysteries, and Super Mysteries along with your favorite Baby-sitters Club books!

BSC Super Specials

BSC Mysteries

More titles ➡

The Baby-sitters Club books continued...

Now THE BABY-SITTERS CLUB®

★ is a Video Club too! ★

What's the scoop with Dawn, Kristy, Mallory, and the other girls?

Be the first to know with G★I★R★L★ magazine!

Hey, Baby-sitters Club readers! Now you can be the first on the block to get in on the action of G★I★R★L★ It's an exciting new magazine that lets you dig in and read...

★ Upcoming selections from Ann Martin's Baby-sitters Club books
★ Fun articles on handling stress, turning dreams into great careers, making and keeping best friends, and much more
★ Plus, all the latest on new movies, books, music, and sports!

To get in on the scoop, just cut and mail this coupon today. And don't forget to tell all your friends about G★I★R★L★ magazine!

A neat offer for you...6 issues for only $15.00.

Sign up today -- this special offer ends July 1, 1996!

❏ **YES!** Please send me G★I★R★L★ magazine. I will receive six fun-filled issues for only $15.00. Enclosed is a check (no cash, please) made payable to G★I★R★L★ for $15.00.

Just fill in, cut out, and mail this coupon with your payment of $15.00 to: G★I★R★L★, c/o Scholastic Inc., 2931 East McCarty Street, Jefferson City, MO 65101.

Name _____

Address _____

City, State, ZIP _____

9013